INFINITY and Me

Kundalini Yoga as Taught by Yogi Bhajan

Compiled and Illustrated by: Harijot Kaur Khalsa

Yogi Bhajan Photo by: Satsimran Kaur

Desktop Production: Khalsa Design Group

Published by: Kundalini Research Institute, Espanola, New Mexico
Copyright Yogi Bhajan, 2004. No portion of this manual may be reproduced without the express written permission of the author.
Please direct your inquiries to: KRI at PO Box 1819, Santa Cruz, NM 87567 or see www.kriteaching.org.

Acknowledgement

The technology of Kundalini Yoga was brought to the West from India by the grace of the Siri Singh Sahib, Harbhajan Singh Khalsa Yogiji (Yogi Bhajan). The teachings in this manual are entirely his gift. We gratefully acknowledge his gift and inspiration to serve our highest human potential. Any errors or omissions in this manual are entirely the fault of the Editors and the Illustrator and by no means reflect upon the perfection and comprehensiveness of the teachings.

Many years ago, a devoted student named Siri Ved Singh Khalsa made a commitment to follow Yogi Bhajan all over the world to record all of his public lectures and classes. Today, because of this commitment, we have thousands of hours of Yogi Bhajan's recorded teachings to experience and to share. May Siri Ved Singh be blessed and remembered for all time for this great good deed.

INTRODUCTION

For Beginners...

If you are a beginning student of Kundalini Yoga, practicing for less than six months, or if you have been practicing without the aid of a certified 3HO Foundation teacher, please read this introduction before you begin to practice from this instruction manual.

Sadhana Guidelines

This manual has been prepared as a supplement and extension to <u>Sadhana Guidelines</u>, in which Yogi Bhajan, who brought the science of Kundalini Yoga to the West, explains yoga, meditation, and the Kundalini. Also important for beginners are the descriptions of the basics of Kundalini Yoga: asanas (postures), mudras (hand positions), bhandas (energy locks), and mantras (sound currents) written by Gurucharan Singh Khalsa. For copies of this manual contact:
Ancient Healing Ways, P.O. Box 130, Espanola, NM 87532, 1-800-359-2940, www.a-healing.com

The Teacher

Kundalini Yoga is a spiritual discipline which cannot be practiced without a teacher. However, it is not necessary for the teacher to be physically present when you practice. To establish a creative link with the Master of Kundalini Yoga, Yogi Bhajan, be sure to tune in to his energy flow using the Adi Mantra, "Ong Namo Guru Dev Namo."

Tuning In

Every Kundalini Yoga session begins with chanting the Adi Mantra: "Ong Namo Guru Dev Namo." By chanting it in proper form and consciousness, the student becomes open to the higher self, the source of all guidance, and accesses the protective link between himself or herself and the divine teacher.

How to recite the Adi Mantra:

Sit in a comfortable cross–legged position with the spine straight. Place the palms of the hands together as if in prayer, with the fingers pointing straight up, and then press the joints of the thumbs into the center of the chest, at the sternum. Inhale deeply. Focus your concentration at the third–eye point. As you exhale, chant the entire mantra in one breath. If your breath is not capable of this, take a quick sip of air through the mouth after "Ong Namo" and then chant the rest of the mantra, extending the sound as long as possible. The sound "Dev" is chanted a minor third higher than the other sounds of the mantra.

As you chant, vibrate the cranium with the sound to create a mild pressure at the third–eye point. Chant this mantra at least three times before beginning your Kundalini Yoga practice.

Pronunciation

The "O" sound in Ong is long, as in "go" and of short duration. The "ng" sound is long and produces a definite vibration on the roof of the mouth and the cranium. The first part of Namo, is short and rhymes with "hum." The "O", as in "go" is held longer. The first syllable of Guru is pronounced as in the word, "good." The second syllable rhymes with "true." The first syllable is short and the second one long. The word Dev rhymes with "gave."

Definition

Ong is the infinite creative energy experienced in manifestation and activity. It is a variation of the cosmic syllable "Om" which denotes God in His absolute or unmanifested state. God as Creator is called Ong.

Namo has the same root as the Sanskrit word Namaste which means reverent greetings. Namaste is a common greeting in India, accompanied by the palms pressed together at the chest or forehead. It implies bowing down. Together Ong Namo means "I call on the infinite creative consciousness," and opens you to the universal consciousness that guides all action.

Guru is the embodiment of the wisdom that one is seeking. The Guru is the giver of the technology. Dev means higher, subtle, or divine. It refers to the spiritual realms. Namo, in closing the mantra, reaffirms the humble reverence of the student. Taken together, Guru Dev Namo means, "I call on the divine wisdom," whereby you bow before your higher self to guide you in using the knowledge and energy given by the cosmic self.

Mental Focus

The following pages contain many wonderful techniques. To fully appreciate and receive the benefits of each one you will need mental focus. Unless you are directed to do otherwise, focus your concentration on the brow point, which is located between the eyebrows at the root of the nose, the third eye point. With your eyes closed, mentally locate this point by turning your eyes gently upwards and inwards. Remain aware of your breath, your body posture, your movements, and any mantra you may be using, even as you center your awareness at the place of focus.

Linking the Breath With a Mantra

A mantra is a sequence of sounds designed to direct the mind by their rhythmic repetition. To fully utilize the power of mantra, link the mantra with your breath cycle. A common mantra is "Sat Nam" (rhymes with "But Mom"). Sat Nam means "Truth is my identity." Mentally repeat "Sat" as you inhale, and "Nam" as you exhale. In this way you filter your thoughts so that each thought has a positive resolution. Mantra makes it easier to keep up during strenuous exercises and adds depth to the performance of even the simplest ones.

Pacing Yourself

Kundalini yoga exercises may involve rhythmic movement between two or more postures. Begin slowly, keeping a steady rhythm. Increase speed gradually, being careful not to strain. Usually the more you practice an exercise, the faster you can go. Just be sure that the spine has become warm and flexible before attempting rapid movements. It is important to be aware of your body and to be responsible for its well-being.

Concluding an Exercise

Unless otherwise stated, an exercise is concluded by inhaling and holding the breath briefly. While the breath is being held, apply the mulbandha or root lock, contracting the muscles around the sphincter, the sex organs, and the navel point. Then exhale and relax. This consolidates the effects of any exercise and circulates the energy to your higher centers. Do not hold the breath to the point of dizziness. If you start to feel dizzy or faint, immediately exhale and relax.

Relaxation Between Exercises

An important part of any exercise is the relaxation following it. Unless otherwise specified, you should allow one to three minutes of relaxation in Easy Pose or lying on the back in Corpse Pose after each exercise. The less experienced you are or the more strenuous the exercise, the longer the relaxation period should be. Some sets end with a period of "deep relaxation" which may extend from three to eleven minutes.

Music

Because of the emphasis on the integration of exercise, meditation, and rhythm in Kundalini Yoga, you will find specific music and mantra tapes used during the exercises. We recommend using the same tapes when you practice because they were chosen by Yogi Bhajan with precise effects in mind. If you don't have the specific tape used in a set, you may do the set without music or substitute other meditative music.

The Fingers

In the Yogic tradition each of the fingers relates to a different planetary energy. Through the positioning of these fingers in mudras one can either draw a specific energy into the body, project it out from the body, or combine it with the energies of other fingers to create a desired effect. The little finger is the Mercury finger and it channels communication. The ring finger is the Sun finger and it channels physical vitality. The middle finger is the Saturn finger and it channels emotion. The index finger is the Jupiter finger and it channels wisdom. The thumb represents one's ego or id.

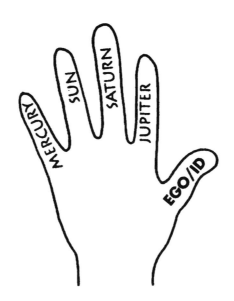

On Your Way...

The exercises in this manual are designed to be safe for most people provided the instructions are followed carefully. The benefits attributed to these exercises come from the centuries-old Yogic tradition. Results will vary due to physical differences and the correctness and frequency of practice. The publishers and authors disclaim all liability in connection with the use of the information in individual cases. As with all unsupervised exercise programs, your use of the instructions in this manual is taken at your own risk. If you have any doubts as to the suitability of the exercises, please consult a doctor.

We invite you to enjoy the practice of the Kundalini yoga techniques contained in the following pages. If you have any questions or concerns about your practice of Kundalini Yoga, please contact your local 3HO Foundation teaching center, listed in the yellow pages or contact the International Kundalini Yogi Teachers' Association (IKYTA) at tel. 505-753-0423 or via Internet at Website: www.yogibhajan.com.

For information on courses and events world-wide, please contact the 3HO Events Office toll free number 888-346-2420.

VII

"When I call on my Infinity, I can come through anything. Then I shall never be handicapped. That is the rule of life. That is how we shall enter the Age of Aquarius."

Yogi Bhajan

Table of Contents

Yoga Sets

A Basic Set	1
A Very Subtle Exercise	6
Adjusting the Navel	7
Balancing the Depository System	11
Building Strength and Vigor	15
Become Strong as Steel	17
Connect Physical and Heavenly Reality	21
Create Muscular Balance	22
Correct Nerve Shallowness	23
Creating Magnetic Fields	25
Experiencing the Pranic and Physical Bodies	28
Eliminate Gastric and Heart Problems	31
Folding and Unfolding of the Energy	33
Kriya for Achieving Comfortable Happy Sleep	36
Move the Glandular System	39
Refreshing the Nervous System	41
Work on the Meridians	44
Ribcage, Lungs, and Lymphatic System	47
Working the Command Post Area	49

Meditations

Mantra to Open Up Blockages in Your Life	51
Mudra to Open Up Blockages in Communication	52
Knowing What To Do	53
Sahaj Yoga	54
Mantra to Make the Blind See	55
Balancing the Projection With the Intention	56
Sa-Ta-Na-Ma 2nd Phase	57
Panj Graani Kriya	59
Prosperity, Fulfillment, Success	60
Pranic Meditation for the Heart Center	61
Working on the Third Chakra	63
Working on the Fourth, Fifth, & Sixth Chakras	64
The Magic Mantra	65
Meditation With the Magic Mantra	66
Using the Magic Mantra as a Gudtkaa	67
Gudtkaa Kriya	68
Maha Gyan Agni Kriya	69

Mantras

Mantras	70

A Basic Set

March 17, 1984

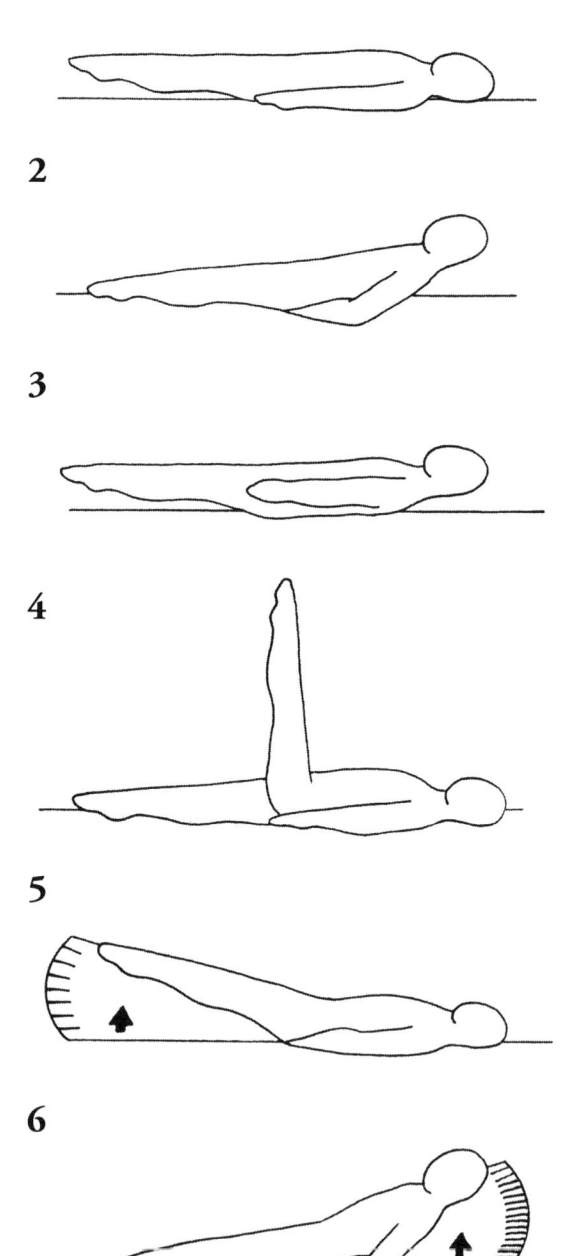

1. Lie down flat on your back with your arms on the floor by your sides. Put your heels together, raise them up exactly six inches, and hold them there. Keep the neck and shoulders on the floor. Keep the spine totally relaxed. 1 1/2 Minutes.

2. Still on your back, put your hands under your buttocks, lift your chest, ground your weight through your pelvic bone, and raise your head and shoulders off the floor a "little bit." This position pressurizes the lymph glands to work on your behalf. 1 Minute.

3. Come into Stretch Pose with your arms parallel to your body and your fingers pointing toward your toes. Breathe long, slow, and deep. The navel will shake if you are in the correct position. Let it do so, feel positive, and keep up. 2 Minutes.

4. Lie on your back and lift your left leg up to ninety degrees. Keep your knees straight and hold this position for 1 1/2 Minutes.
Change legs, lifting the right leg up to ninety degrees. Hold the position for 1 Minute.

5. Lie on your back with your legs straight, your heels together, and your hands under your buttocks. Raise both your legs up one inch at a time. The first time, lift them to the count of 12 movements up (about 20 seconds) and 12 movements down (about 20 seconds). The second time, raise them in ten movements up (about 15 seconds) and lower them in ten movements (about 15 seconds). The third time raise the legs in ten movements (about 10 seconds) hold the top position for 15 seconds and lower the legs in 10 movements (about 5 seconds). For the last time go up to a count of eight (about 8 seconds), mentally chanting "Har" at the navel point with each inch, hold the position at the top of the cycle feeling the mantra "Hari Har" six times at the navel point (about 20 seconds). Then moving down to the mental count of eight repetitions of "Har" (about 8 seconds). Focus on the mantra, considering the navel point as the center of Divine Power.

6. Lie on your back with your hands under your buttocks, raise the shoulders and head in one-inch increments to the count of "Har." Seventeen counts up (about 17 seconds). Hold at the top of the movement and feel "Hari Har" at navel five times (about 10 seconds). Then lower yourself back down in ten one-inch increments to ten counts of "Har" (10 seconds). This exercise sequence is done only one time.

"Normally when you do a good set of Kundalini Yoga, it extends you. It is very good to get extended, because you can use that energy for days and days."

YB

7A

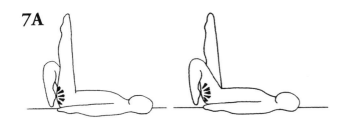

7B

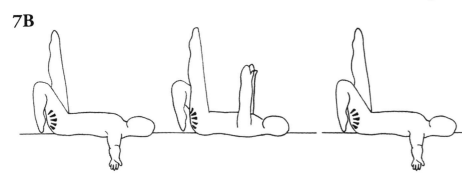

7. To reconcile the energy that you have just created, lie on your back and raise your legs up to ninety degrees:

    A. Begin kicking your buttocks alternately with your heels. 2 Minutes.

    B. Keep kicking your buttocks and bring your arms straight out to the side on the floor. Lift the arms straight up in the air above the body, palms facing each other. Then lower the arms back to the floor. The arms move as if you are clapping, but the hands don't touch. Move rhythmically. Dance your feet and dance your hands. Send a message to the motor system to coordinate the movement. Arms move together, legs move alternately. 6 Minutes.

8. Lie on your back with your legs straight.

    One: raise your arms up to ninety degrees.

    Two: lower your arms to the floor behind your head.

    Three: raise your arms back up to ninety degrees.

    Four: lower your arms down to the floor by your sides and begin the sequence again with "one." Let your arms create a sound each time they hit the floor. Move at a pace of one second or less for each movement. Breathe long and deep. Move rhythmically. 3 1/2 Minutes.

8

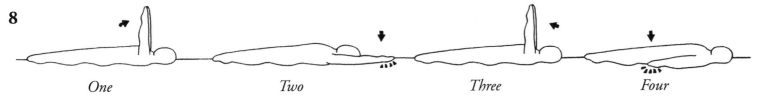

One   *Two*   *Three*   *Four*

9. Still lying on your back with your arms on the floor by your sides.

    One: raise your arms up to ninety degrees.

    Two: bring the arms down to hit the ground behind your head and raise your heels up one inch as your hands hit the ground.

    Three: hold the heels at one inch and bring the arms back to ninety degrees.

    Four: lower the arms and the heels to the floor at the same time. Move at a pace of one second or less for each movement. 3 Minutes

This exercise works the upper and lower glandular systems to a regular count. Normally we get locked down in our pelvic area and the breath becomes smaller and shallower. This breath pattern is a sign of depression. If you can breathe heavily from the navel point, you can get out of depression very fast. People mistakenly think that depression or negativity is a circumstantial mood or mental attitude, they don't understand that it is a physical symptom.

9

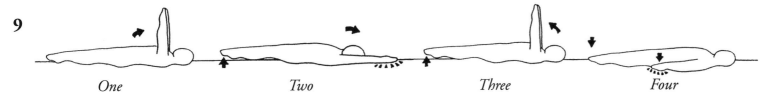

One   *Two*   *Three*   *Four*

10

10. Lie on your back. Interlace your hands behind your head with your elbows out to the sides. Feel depressed. (Create this mental state so you can understand how the organization of your mind and body works. Body and mind are friends, they work together.) Keep your heels together and your legs straight. Raise both legs up to ninety degrees and lower them back to the floor. Continue 1 Minute. One up and down movement takes two to three seconds.

This is the best exercise for the serum of the spine. It gives you "prospective projective sensibility" of almost the entire body.

11

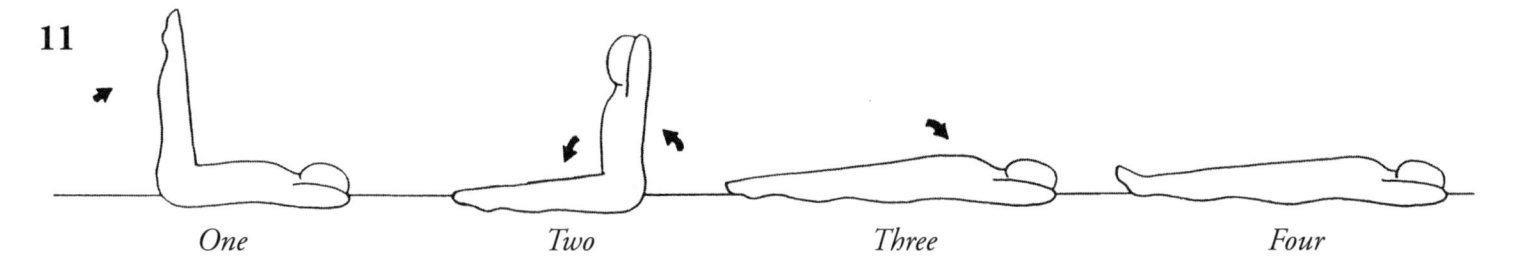

One   Two   Three   Four

11. Lie on back, hands interlaced behind your head.
   One: lift your legs up to ninety degrees.
   Two: lower them, using this downward motion of the legs to powerfully lever yourself up into a sitting position.
   Three: lie back down.
   Four: relax totally, keeping your hands interlaced behind your head. Relax navel and upper lymph area. Start again with "one" and continue the sequence for 4 Minutes.

This exercise activates the lymph area and combines it with the navel. This wonderful combination can protect you from a lot of unhealthy things.

12

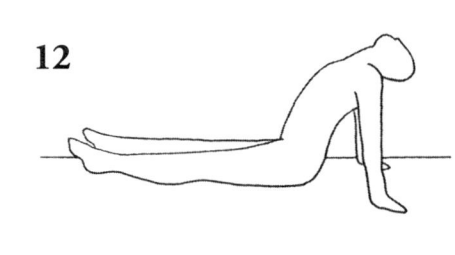

12. Sitting straight with your legs extended, place your hands on the floor in line with your shoulders and arch the shoulders and head into a quarter circle. The chest is lifted and the head hangs back. Keep a balanced backward stretch, do not compress the neck or lower spine. 1 1/2 Minutes. For the last 10 seconds do Breath of Fire and pump the navel.

13. Lie on your back and place your hands under your neck, holding it tightly. Move the pelvis, turning it to the left and stretching, then turning it to the right and stretching. 2 1/2 Minutes.

13

14

14. Lie on your back and place your hands beneath your lower back, under your navel. Extend the left leg out straight (parallel to the floor, but not touching it) as you pull the right knee to your chest. Then extend the right leg out straight (parallel to the floor, but not touching it) as you pull the left knee to your chest. Legs move in and out like pistons. Breathe with the movement. 1 Minute.

15. Stand up straight, raise your hands over your head, and jump up and down quickly and rhythmically (one jump per second). 2 Minutes.

15

16. Stand up straight, spread your legs wide apart. Put your hands on your waist. Keep your spine straight throughout this movement. The pace is one movement per second.
    One: bend to the left bringing your forehead toward your left knee.
    Two: come standing up straight.
    Three: bend to the right, bringing your forehead toward your right knee.
    Four: come standing up straight. 1 Minute.

17. In the same position as exercise sixteen, widen your legs further. Keep your spine straight, bend forward so that your hands touch the ground between your legs, and let your body hang. 1 Minute.
Stay in the position, begin Breath of Fire, wink your eyes as fast as you can, and shake your hips as fast as you can. 1 Minute.

16

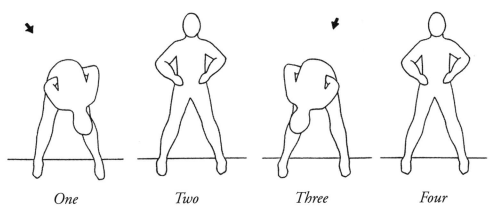

One   Two   Three   Four

17

18

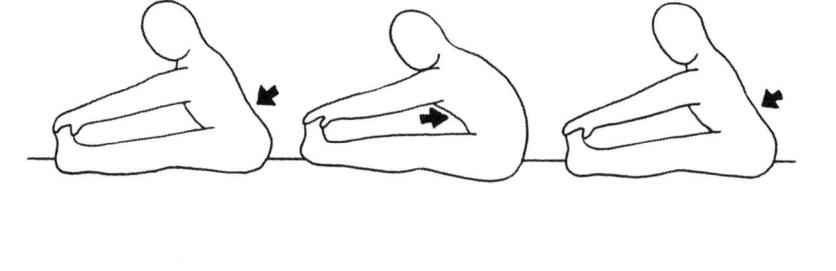

19 & 20

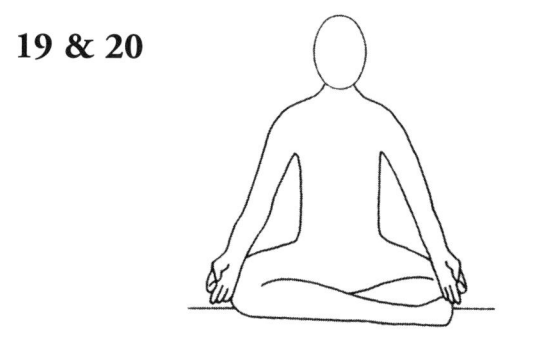

21

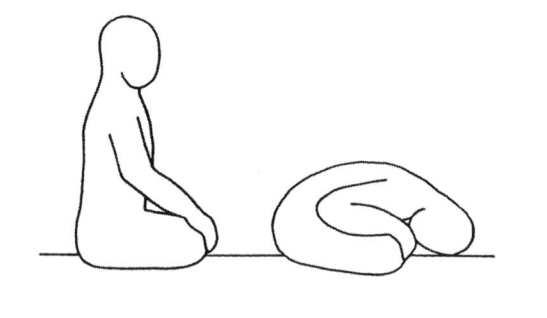

18. Sit straight with your legs stretched out in front of you. Reach forward and catch your toes with both hands. Keep your head up and keep it steady. Begin spinal flexes in the area between your shoulders and lower back. Keep your knees straight but not locked. Really move the back ribs. 1 1/2 Minutes.

19. Sit in Easy Pose with your eyes closed. Musically chant the *Sarb Shakti Mantra*: Gobinday, Mukanday, Udaaray, Apaaray, Hareeung, Kareeung, Nirnaamay, Akaamay. 2 1/2 Minutes. Then continue chanting, while pulling the navel at each sacred word. 4 Minutes.

20. In the same position, go into silence and pray that you may be healthy, happy, holy, prosperous, and good. Any good word that you can think of, say it to yourself. List all goodness. I am kind. I am beautiful. I am wonderful. I am positive. I am healthy. I am happy. I am holy. I am graceful. Anything you can count which is positive or could be positive. Give yourself positive affirmations. (Fully concentrate. This mental exercise is as much a yoga exercise as any of the previous physical exercises.) 1 1/2 Minutes.

21. Still in Easy Pose, say a positive affirmation to yourself eight times and bend forward to bring your forehead to the floor in salutation, making an affirmation to the Lord of the Universe. (for a total of nine affirmations) Then rise up. Continue this cycle using a new affirmation each time and repeat this whole sequence a total of five times.

22. Relax.

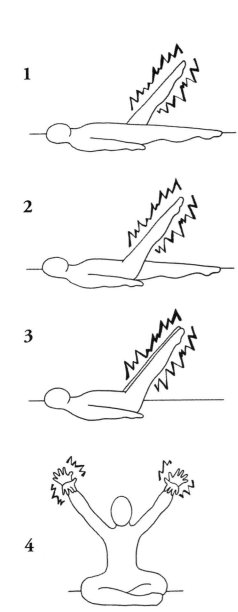

A Very Subtle Exercise
Getting to the Root of Sub-conscious Depression
February 20, 1985

1. Lie down flat on your back, with your arms by your sides, and raise your left leg up to sixty degrees. Shake your left leg vigorously while simultaneously relaxing the rest of your body. Keep your knee straight and shake your leg really hard. 3 Minutes. You are totally reorganizing the stimulation of every gland in the body.

2. Lie down flat on your back and raise your right leg up to sixty degrees. Shake your right leg vigorously while simultaneously relaxing the rest of your body. Do not let the knees bend, keep both legs straight. You must shake your right leg physically harder than you shook your left leg. The shaking of the right side must be very intense. 3 Minutes.

3. Lie down flat on your back, with your arms by your sides, and raise both legs up to sixty degrees. Vigorously shake them both at the same time, but keep your knees straight. 3 Minutes.

4. Sit in Easy Pose, raise both arms straight up, and vigorously shake your hands moving from the wrists. The wrists and the hands both move. The elbows are kept straight. Close your eyes and concentrate on the pineal gland by focusing your internal gaze at the top center of your head. Meditate deeply, listening to the tape *You Are My Lover, Lord* (Available from Ancient Healing Ways AHW#16386). Listen from your ears to your pineal gland. 7 1/2 Minutes.

5. Put your hands in your lap and continue to meditatively listen to the tape. Breathe long and slow and deep with your eyes closed. Continue to the end of the tape (approximately 9 Minutes more). Inhale, sit straight, and meditate, as you hold your breath for one minute (or the maximum time you can hold your breath up to one minute). Don't over-pressure yourself while holding the breath. Exhale like cannon fire and hold the breath out for 30 seconds (or to your maximum up to 30 seconds) while you powerfully and continuously pull in on the navel. Inhale and relax.

   To make long-term positive changes in your life, do this kriya every morning for one week. During this one week, a feeling of rhythm in the sciatica will develop…it will become heavier and heavier and more positive. You will sweat. In the morning, after you do this exercise, write down the time of day and how you feel. In the evening write down the time of day and your assessment of how your day went. Write down how you feel you are being changed by this meditation practice. Keep this record and assess it after the week is over.

"Life starts from that day when you realize who you are. From that day onward, you want to build who you should be. When you have built to the extent that you are who you should be, from then onward, you have the right to overflow, to share… First there has to be a glass. Second it has to be filled. Third, then it can overflow. These are the three known stages."

YB

Adjusting the Navel

April 18, 1984

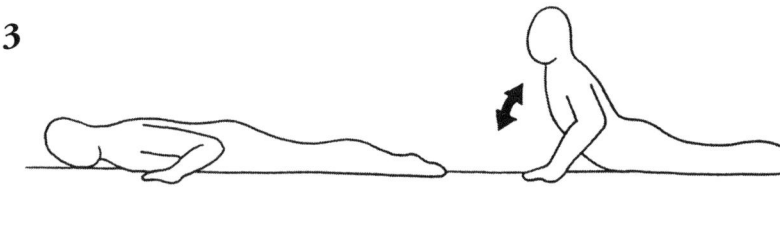

Assess you own energy before you begin this set, so that you can re-assess your energy once you have completed it. This will help you to better appreciate and understand the effects of Kundalini Yoga.

1. Lie down flat on your back, bend your right knee, and use both arms to lock the right knee against your chest. Hold the right leg stable in this position and don't let it move.

Begin to raise and lower the left leg, with powerful long, deep breathing. Your breathing should be loud enough to hear. Move the left leg powerfully and quickly. One up and down movement of the leg should take only two seconds. Keep your face serene. This action will adjust your navel point, providing the bent leg is kept stable. 4 Minutes.

2. Switch sides and continue the exercise. 1 1/2 Minutes.

3. Lie down flat on your stomach with your chin touching the ground. Place your hands under your ribcage. Press your palms against the ground, arching up to raise your ribcage and head off the ground. Then lower your body down, bringing your chin (the moon center) back to the ground. Move quickly between these two positions. The chin touches the ground each time you come down. The pace is one lift and return cycle per second. Continue for 2 1/2 Minutes. This exercise automatically adjusts the neck and the ribcage.

4. Lie on your stomach. Balance yourself on your chest and chin. Bend your knees and raise your buttocks up into the air. Reach back and grab the backs of your knees with your hands. Bend your lower back. Don't allow it to arch upward. Find a position that is balanced with no strain on any part of your body. Let your body relax to its own adjustment. 2 Minutes. This posture is to remove wind that is locked inside, poisoning your system.

"The beauty of Kundalini Yoga is that if one set is done A to Z for plus or minus three minutes, it totally re-invigorates your whole system. It brings to you all energy and all balance to prana and apana. There are twenty-two forms of yoga and they all lead to one thing: raising the Kundalini. Purpose of raising the Kundalini is not that we start flying in the air and all those gimmicks. When the Kundalini is raised, a person is super alert to everything.

5

5. Lie down on your stomach and grab the upper part of your feet near the toes. Press your feet away from your body, lifting up into Bow Pose. Then relax down and lift up again. The pace is one up and down cycle per second. Continue this up and down motion for 2 Minutes. This exercise can take away inches from the sides, removing "love handles."

6

6. Still lying on your stomach, begin kicking your buttocks with alternate heels. Kick hard. Keep your chin on the ground. 1 Minute.

7

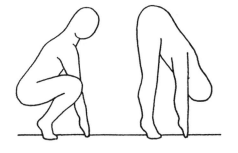

7. Come squatting on your heels in Frog Pose. Inhale and straighten your legs, keeping the fingertips touching the ground between your knees. Exhale and come back to the squatting position. Keep your heels together as you move up and down. The pace is fast, one second per up and down movement. Do 52 Frogs.

8. Lie on your back with your hands under your head. Lock your elbows up by your ears. Keep your heels together. Raise both legs up to ninety degrees and lower them back to the floor. The pace is one second to raise the legs up and one second to lower them down. Continue for 1 1/2 Minutes.

8

9. Lie flat on your back. Relax your body with your arms by your sides. Use your tongue to make a rapid ululation: La-la-la-la-la-la-la-la-la-la-la-la-la-la-la. 1 Minute. (Mostly our tongues are stiff. Flexibility of the tongue is important for getting maximum benefit from chanting.)

One becomes an acknowledged human being in every field of life one touches. It is for the householder. It allows us to marry and have children. You can take your life pressure absolutely nicely and still be young, beautiful, healthy, and able to keep going. That is the purpose...It is a very day to day, living experience. With all our mistakes and with all our weaknesses, still we can make ourselves healthy, happy, and holy. That is the purpose."

YB

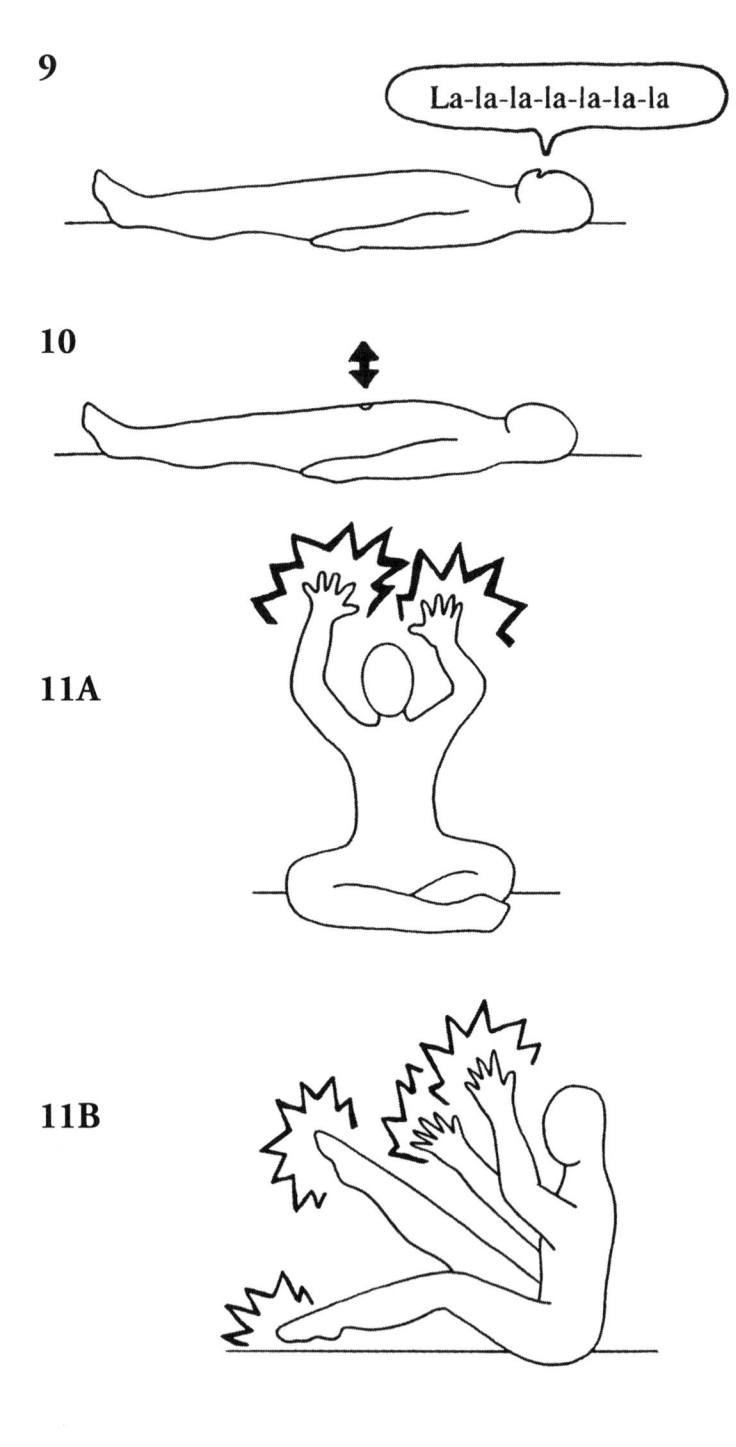

10. Remain lying on your back. Rest your hands by your sides. Begin to pump the navel in and out. 10 Seconds. Then continue to pump the navel and use the tongue to continuously chant "Har, Har, Har, Har, Har, Har." The pace is two Har's per second. Connect the action of the tip of the tongue with the action of the navel point. Move the navel powerfully. Keep the body lying flat on the floor; have no tension in any part of your body other than the navel. 3 Minutes.

This exercise, practiced correctly, can give you long life, new energy, and the return of youth. It renews the cells and is the best facial you can give yourself. If you regularly practice it for ten to fifteen minutes a day, you will stay youthful and can avoid many health problems.

11. Sit in easy pose and raise your arms up over your head.
    A. Begin shaking and moving your whole body from the waist up. Create a very relaxed, very active movement. Let yourself go, make every movement unfamiliar and unique. Do not repeat patterns of movement. This totally relaxed, free style movement is called a "sitting dance." Continue for 1 Minute.
    B. Now remain sitting, keep moving the upper body, and add the legs to the sitting dance. Everything should move in your own unique rhythm but you must remain sitting. Be very relaxed. 1 Minute.

12

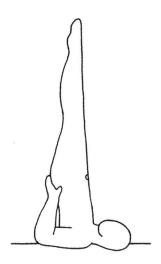

13

12. Come into Shoulder Stand. Keep your legs very straight, Chant: "Hari Raam, Hari Raam, Hari Raam, Haray, Haray," This is a navel point mantra. Each repetition takes approximately five seconds. Hold the position and chant for 1 1/2 Minutes.

13. Sit comfortably and meditate like a yogi. Pretend to be nice and become thoughtless. Say "no" to every thought. Let no thought pass through you. Create the thought form that "you have no thought." 3 Minutes.

Begin chanting long Sat Naam's. The ratio of this chant is eight beats of "Sat" to one beat of "Naam." In other words, the length of time you chant "Sat" is eight times longer than the length of time you chant "Naam." 1 Minute. (This is approximately 20 seconds per repetition of the mantra.)

14. Relax. Feel yourself. Assess how differently you feel now from how you felt before you started this set.

Balancing the Depository System

May 2, 1984

1. Stand up and bend over at the waist, keeping your spine straight and parallel to the floor. Let the arms hang down loosely with no stiffness. Use the power of the body to swing the arms from side to side, like a pendulum. Don't make an effort to move the arms. 2 1/2 Minutes.

2. Still standing in the same position, with the arms hanging loosely, twist from the base of your spine to swing the arms up as high as you can on each side. Keep going, this exercise puts pressure on your muscles but they will adjust. 3 Minutes. Move rhythmically.

3. Lie down on your stomach and lock your hands behind your lower back. Inhale through your nose, pull your shoulder blades down your back and lift your chest and head off the floor. Exhale through your mouth as you lower your chest back to the floor and raise your arms up as in Yoga Mudra. Inhale and continue. 3 Minutes. When done correctly, this exercise releases deposits in the shoulders.

4. Lie down on your back and raise your legs up straight. Catch your toes with your hands. Hold this position for 30 seconds. Then, from this position, inhale and pull your legs back over into Plough Pose. Exhale and return to the starting position. Continue moving from position to position for 2 1/2 Minutes. Move with a breath rhythm so that the kidneys can have a soothing massage.

"Try to become part of the exercise. Exercising IS meditating at the same time."

YB

5

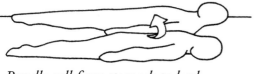
Bundle roll from stomach to back

Bundle roll from back to stomach

5. Lie on your stomach, make your spine straight, press your legs together, and press your arms into your sides. Bundle Roll from your stomach onto your back. Then do Bundle Roll from your back onto your stomach. Roll back and forth but stay in one spot. 3 1/2 Minutes. This exercise can adjust the whole body. Move quickly and powerfully.

6

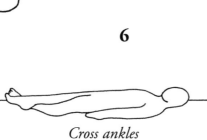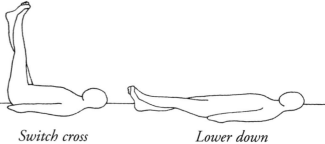

Cross ankles *Raise legs* *Switch cross* *Lower down*

6. Lie on your back and cross your legs at the ankles. Keep the ankles crossed and raise your legs up straight. Reverse the cross at the ankles and lower your legs. Continue for 5 Minutes. Move quickly.

7. Squat down in Frog Pose, letting the arms hang loosely for 30 Seconds. From this position, slowly rise up to standing, keeping the arms hanging loosely. Then slowly lower back down into the squatting position. 1 1/2 Minutes. Move slowly without pressure. Use your thighs to rise up and your calves to lower down.

8. Stand up and bend forward bringing your hands to the floor. Raise your left leg as high as it will go, keeping your knee straight. Hold this position for 30 Seconds. Then begin lifting each leg alternately up as high as you can. Keep your knees straight. Move fast for 1 Minute.

7

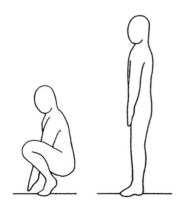

8

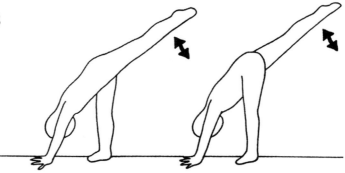

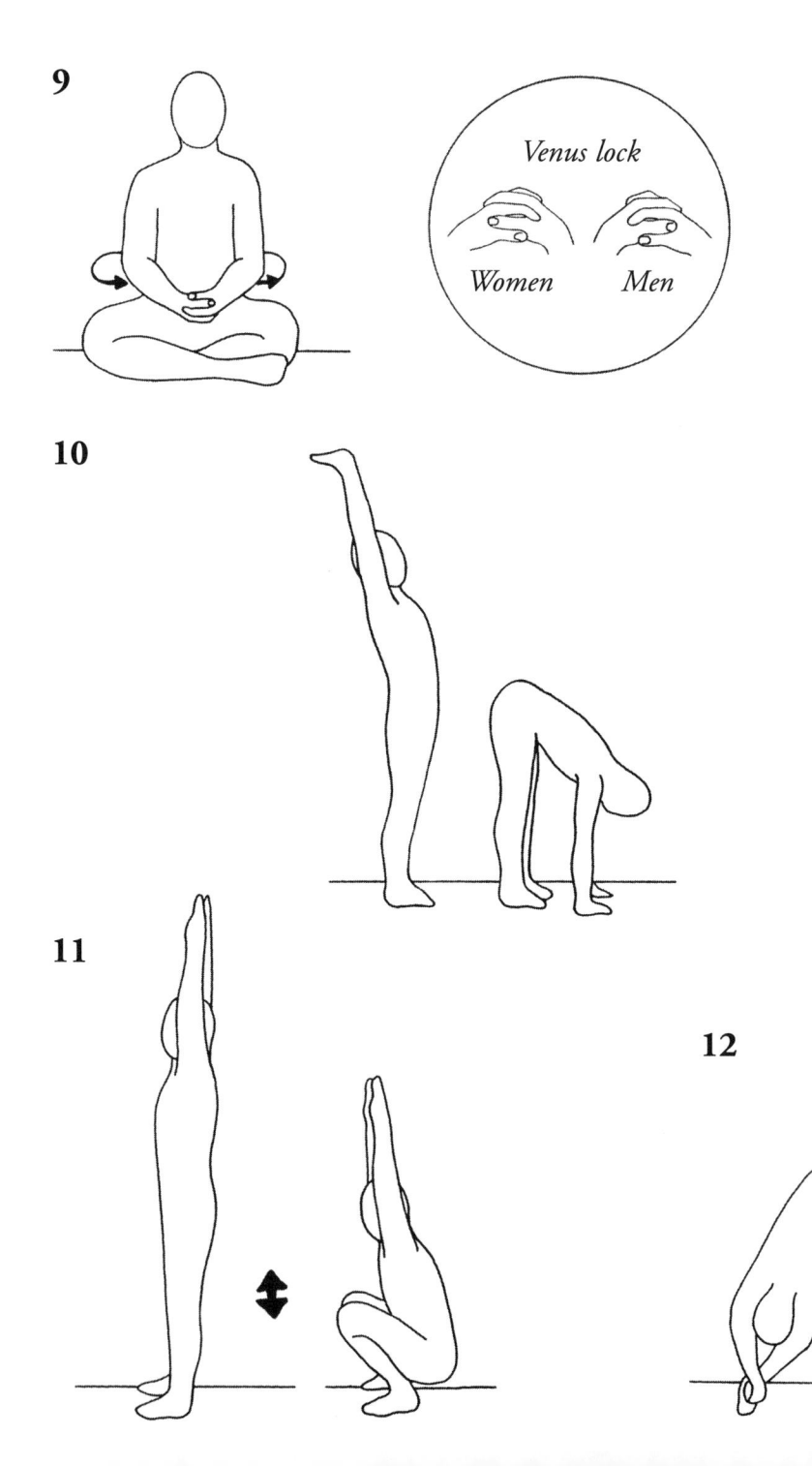

9

Venus lock

Women *Men*

10

11

12

Mudra

9. Sit in Easy Pose with your hands in Venus Lock in your lap. Rotate the upper body in a backward circle moving counter-clockwise. 1 Minute.

10. Stand up straight with your arms up over your head. Bend forward, touch the floor, and rise back up. Move at a pace of two seconds down and two seconds up. 1 Minute.

11. Stand up straight with your arms up over your head. Squat down into Crow Pose and rise back up. 30 Seconds. Move at a pace of two seconds down and two seconds up.

12. Stand up with your feet spread wide apart. Stretch your arms out straight with the backs of the hands facing each other. Then cross the right wrist over the left so that the palms are facing each other and interlock your fingers. Keep your arms in this lock. Inhale and raise your arms up over your head. Exhale and bend to the right to touch your toes. Inhale back up straight. Exhale and bend to the left to touch your toes. Continue bending alternately to each side for 1 1/2 Minutes. The pace is rapid: one to two seconds on each side.

13

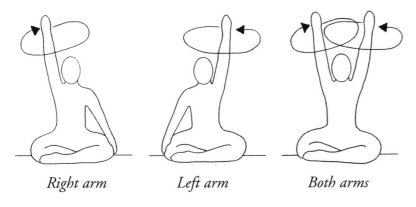

Right arm   *Left arm*   *Both arms*

14

15

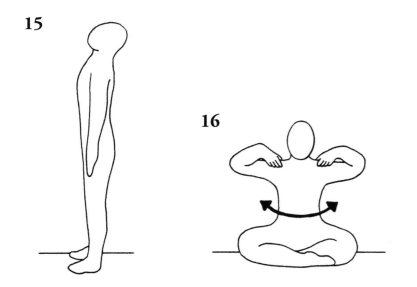

16

17

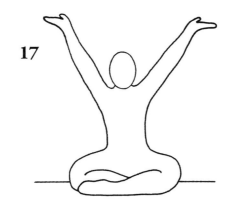

13. Sit down and raise your right arm up as straight as you can. Rotate it in a one to two foot circle over your head. 30 Seconds. Change arms and rotate your left arm in a circle over your head. 15 Seconds. Rotate both arms in alternate circles over your head. 1 1/2 Minutes. Move powerfully.

14. Sitting in Easy Pose, bend forward to rest on your elbows. Begin hitting the ground with alternate palms. Move powerfully. 1 Minute.

15. Stand up, lower your shoulder blades and raise your chest. Raise your chin up and let your head fall backward. Inhale deeply and exhale completely in this position 4 times (about 10 seconds for each breath).

16. In Easy Pose, put your hands on your shoulders, fingers in front, thumbs behind. Twist to the left and chant "Har." Twist to the right and chant "Haree." 2 1/2 Minutes.
Move quickly and remember that you are chanting God's name.

17. Raise your arms up to sixty degrees, palms facing toward the sky. Concentrate at the third eye point. Chant "Har, Har, Wha Hay Guroo" in a monotone for 1 Minute. (One repetition is about 2 seconds.)
    Inhale, hold the breath for 15 Seconds as you chant mentally. Exhale. Inhale, hold the breath, and mentally chant for 15 Seconds. Exhale, and relax.

Building Strength and Vigor

June 6, 1984 evening class

This is a vigorous set of exercises. Each exercise must be done quickly and powerfully.

1

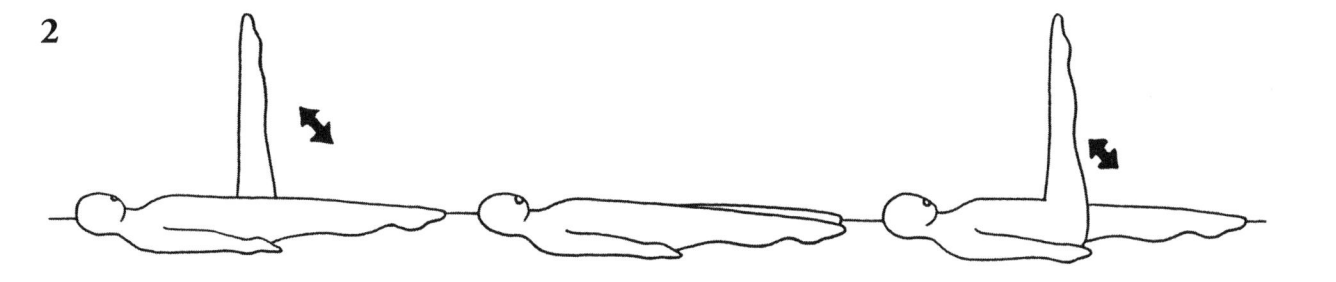

1. Lie on your stomach and grab your ankles. Use your legs to pull against your arms and rise up into Bow Pose. Lower back down. Continue this up and down Bow Pose for 6 Minutes.

"When the spirit flows it will wash away your weaknesses. As long as you have weaknesses, your spirit is not flowing."

YB

2

2. Lie on your back alternately lifting each leg up to ninety degrees. Breathe heavily through the mouth and move fast.
1 1/2 Minutes.

3

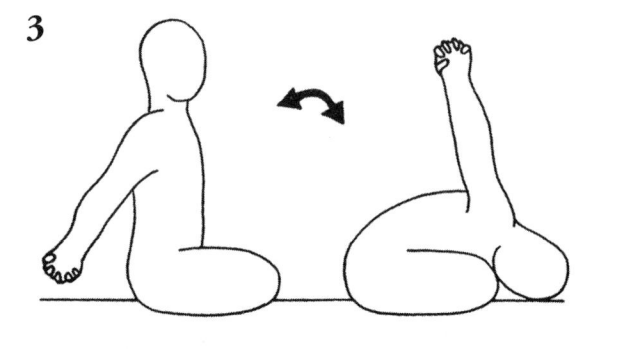

3. Sit in Easy Pose and interlock your hands behind your back. Inhale, keep the breath held, and bow down eight to sixteen times, bringing your forehead to the floor and raising your arms as high as you can with each bow. Exhale. Inhale and continue.
1 1/2 Minutes.

4

4. Raise yourself up slowly into Half Wheel Pose. Hold the position for 30 Seconds. Then begin alternate leg lifts in Half Wheel Pose. 2 Minutes. Done correctly, this exercise has the capacity to take away pain from your life.

5. Sit in Easy Pose and place your hands on top of your head with the fingers interlocked. Twist your torso left and right, while, at the same time, slowly bending forward as far as you can. Move inch by inch. When you have gone as far forward as you can, continue twisting left and right and gradually rise back up and go as far backward as you can. 1 1/2 Minutes.

6. Relax.

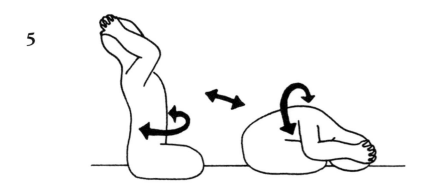

5

1

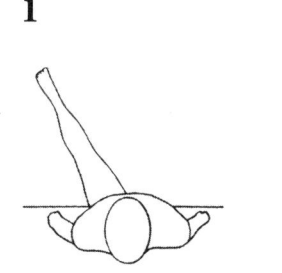 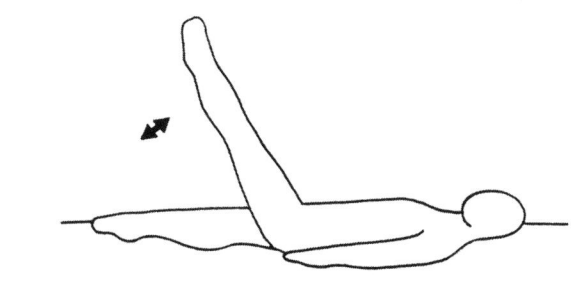

Raise left leg 60° out to the side while you simultaneously raise it 60° up

2

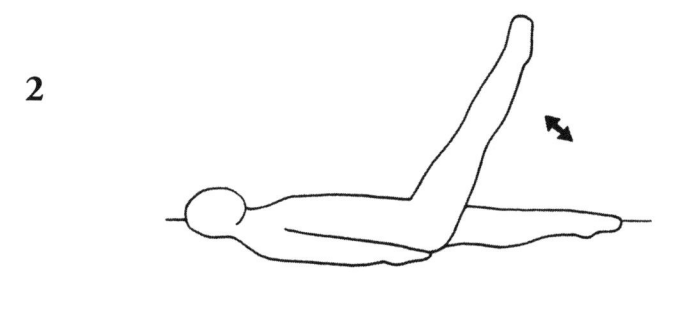

3

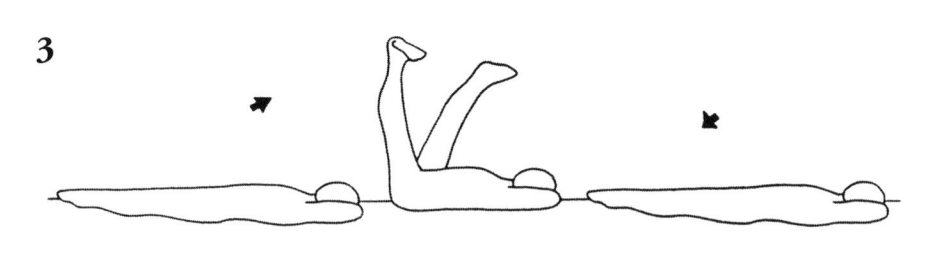

Become Strong as Steel

May 21, 1984

This yoga set is physically demanding, every exercise is to be done with maximum strength and speed.

1. Lie down flat on your back with your hands by your sides. Lift the left leg sixty degrees up from the floor while, at the same time, angling it out to the side at sixty degrees. Then lower it back to the floor. Continue raising and lowering the left leg to these angles. Don't bend your knees, keep both legs straight. Move quickly: up and down should be done in one second. Breathe heavily and push yourself. 3 Minutes.

2. Change legs, raising the right leg up to sixty degrees and out to the side at a sixty-degree angle and then lowering it. Put yourself into the exercise heart and soul. The movement has to be strong, with total tension in the muscles. Keep your legs straight. Move fast with a heavy breath. 2 1/2 Minutes.

3. Still lying on your back with the legs stretched out straight and your heels together. Put your hands under your head. Inhale and lift both legs up to sixty degrees, while at the same time spreading the legs so that each leg is out to the side at sixty degrees. The heels start out together on the ground and the legs open apart as you lift them up and out to the sides. Exhale and lower your legs back down so that the heels come together as your legs touch the floor. Continue this up-as-you-open-your-legs, down-as-you-close-your-legs movement. Move with the breath. Start slowly, but quickly build up to a rapid pace. 2 Minutes.

   In this exercise, the navel will move and the sciatica nerve will stretch.

4. Relax 4 Minutes.

"A master takes little and gives a lot."

YB

5

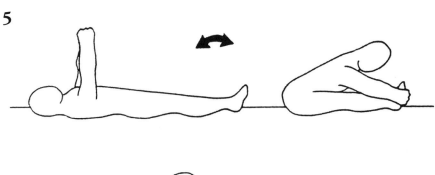

5. Lie on your back. Interlace your fingers and raise your arms up to ninety degrees. Inhale, come sitting up, and bend forward to touch the ground, looping your interlaced hands around your feet. Exhale and lie back down. Move quickly with a strong breath. 2 1/2 Minutes.

6

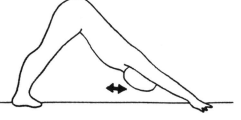

6. Balance on your hands and feet, angling your body into a triangle shape, so that your arms and legs are at a sixty-degree angle to the floor. Create a secure and balanced position. Move so that your upper body comes six inches forward and return to the starting position. Continue rocking forward and back. One forward and back movement takes two seconds. Feet remain stationary. 2 Minutes.

7

7. Come up into Half Wheel Pose. Begin Breath of Fire. Pump your navel; pump it like it's a dancing bird. 1 1/2 Minutes.

8

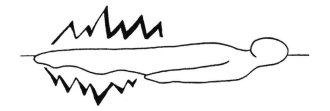

8. Lie flat on your back, with your legs out straight and your heels together. Shake your legs, moving hips, thighs, calves, and feet. Move vigorously and powerfully to refresh the blood supply to your legs. 2 Minutes.

9

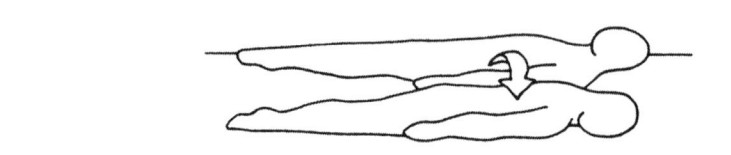

Bundle roll one turn to the left

Bundle roll one turn to the right

10

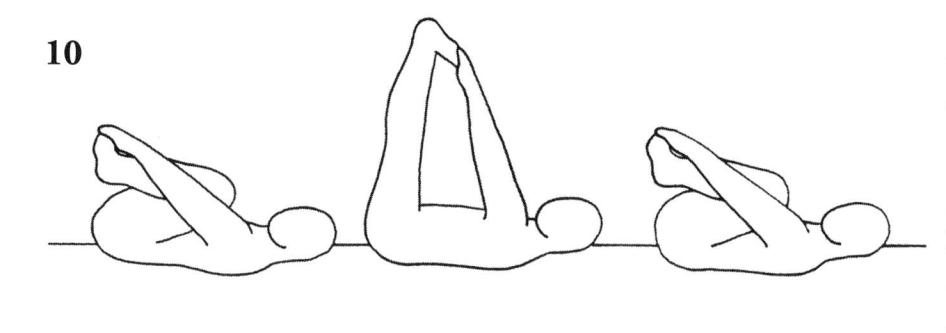

11

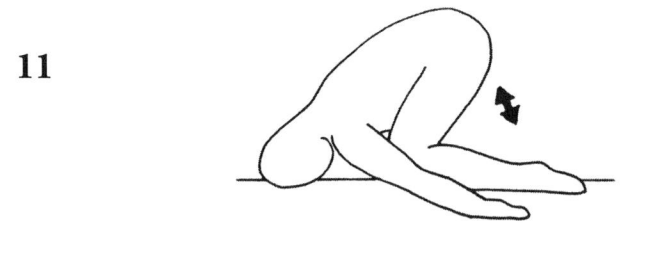

12

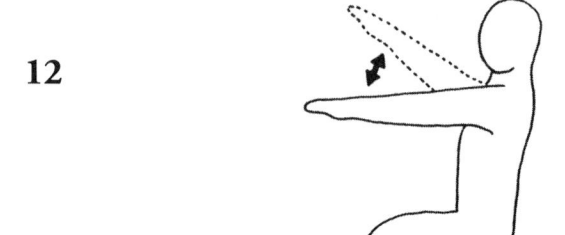

9. Lie on your back with your spine straight, legs together, arms pressing into your sides. Bundle roll from side to side: from the starting position, roll to the left side over onto your stomach. Then roll back to the starting position. Then roll to the right side from your back onto your stomach. Move quickly. Continue 1 1/2 Minutes. This exercise tunes up the whole nervous system.

10. Lie on your back. Bring your knees to your chest and hold onto your toes. Straighten your legs up to ninety degrees and lower them back to your chest. Move like a steam engine up and down. 2 Minutes.

11. Lie down in Baby Pose with your arms by your sides palms up. Lift your buttocks up and down in a fast, hammering motion. This exercise builds your lungs. 3 Minutes.

12. Sit in Easy Pose with your arms stretched out in front parallel to the floor. Keep the chin in and chest out, holding the spine and neck straight. Move the arms up and down in unison. Beat the air with all the strength you have. Keep your arms straight from shoulder to fingertips. You are pumping blood to the brain so the movement must be fast and strong. 3 1/2 Minutes.

13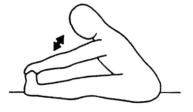

14

15

13. Sit up with your legs stretched out straight. Hold your toes, keeping your spine straight. Bend forward, bringing your chest toward your thighs, and then rise back up, moving quickly. One up and down should take only one second. Get mad and move fast, using your anger to fuel the movement.
1 1/2 Minutes.

14. Sit up with your legs still stretched out straight, heels together and feet flexed. Hold your toes and stretch backward as far as you can. Pump your navel as fast as a rattlesnake can shake its tail. 1 Minute.

15. Sit up straight "like a yogi" with your hands in your lap, palms up, right hand resting in the left hand with the thumbs touching. Rapidly chant "Har, Har, Haree" in a monotone using the tip of the tongue. (One repetition of the mantra takes 1 second.) 2 1/2 Minutes.

Then inhale and hold the breath for 15 seconds and use the tip of the tongue to repeat the mantra *without making any sound*. Inhale again, hold the breath 10 seconds, and relax.

16. Lie down flat on your back with your hands by your sides palms up. Totally relax your body. Concentrate at your third eye point. 8 Minutes. (In class, Yogi Bhajan played a gong meditation to "fly your soul." By listening to this gong meditation while concentrating at the third eye, Yogi Bhajan said that you could become fearless. It is worth acquiring the tape to experience this gong meditation.)

17. Wake yourself up. Move your feet round and round. Move your legs round and round, Move your hips round and round. Move your chest up and down and back and forth. Move your arms round and round. Move your neck round and round and then get up.

1

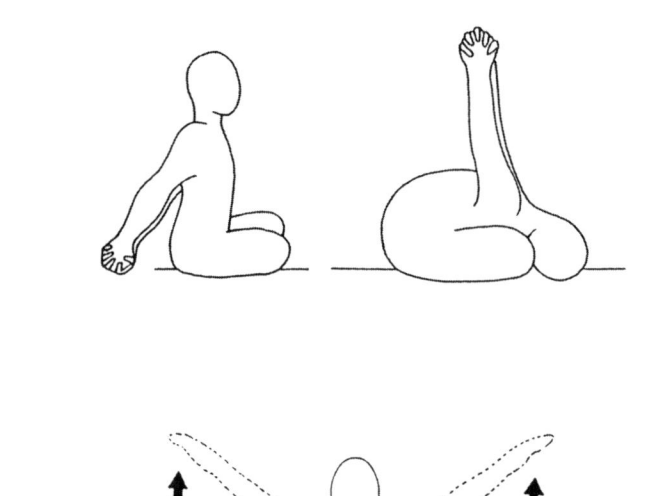

2

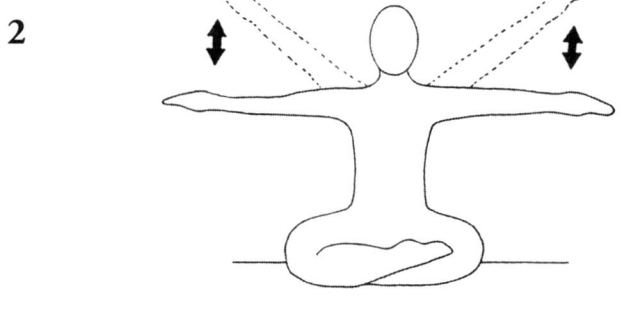

3

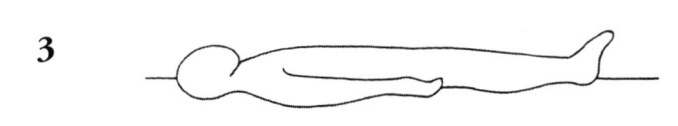

5

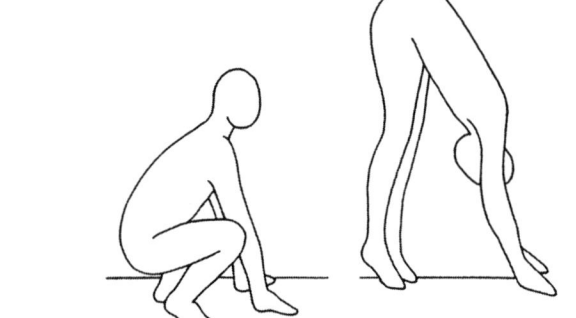

Connecting Physical and Heavenly Reality

January 28, 1986

1. Sit in Easy Pose with your fingers interlaced behind your back. Bend forward, bringing your forehead to the floor, while raising your arms up as high as you can into Yoga Mudra. Keep your elbows straight. Begin Breath of Fire, keeping the breath strong and heavy. It will give you a different dimension. 1 Minute.

Stay in the position, continue the Breath of Fire, and imagine that you are in the presence of God Almighty. Feel the essence of infinite energy. 2 1/2 Minutes.

2. Rise up into Easy Pose. Stretch your arms straight out to the sides. Do not bend your elbows. Begin moving your arms up and down as if you were flying. Begin Breath of Fire. Imagine that you are an eagle flying in the sky viewing the whole universe under your wings. Your imagination must become your reality. Breathe powerfully and fly powerfully. Put all of your energy into it. 3 Minutes.

3. Gong meditation. In order to receive the benefits of this entire set, it is required that this exercise be done with the exact gong meditation that Yogi Bhajan played in class. The tape of this class (KYB 094) is available from Ancient Healing Ways. (See page II.) Lie down straight and put yourself into a deep sleep. Totally space out as you listen to the gong. Concentrate on your navel and project out. The gong will carry you with the sound of the Ultimate, the sound of the universe. 7 Minutes.

4. Inhale deeply and wake up. Rotate your hands and feet. Do Cat Stretch on each side.

5. Come into the squatting position for Frog Pose. Inhale as you straighten your legs and come into the up position of Frog Pose. Chant "Har" as you come back into the squatting position. Continue this movement for 1 Minute.

"You are the best beloved creature created by God in His individual will, but you have not accepted your Self as God within you."

YB

Create Muscular Balance

June 22, 1984

This set will give your muscles a chance to break through their own dogma. Moving in habitual patterns creates an imbalance in our muscles. Over time, some get very strong and some get very weak. This imbalance is the cause of every dis-ease.

1. Sit in Easy Pose and lock your hands behind your neck. Inhale and twist left. Exhale and twist right. Keep your neck straight. Move the torso as one consolidated unit, moving from the base to the top of the head. Move powerfully to bring new blood to your muscles and tissues. 11 Minutes.

2. Sitting on your heels with your arms by your sides. The following movement is done to the rhythm of Ragi Sat Nam Singh's *Jaap Sahib* tape. Set your rhythm with the chanting of "Namastang" as it is chanted in the beginning part of the tape and continue in that rhythm.
    A. When you hear "Namastang" begin bowing your forehead to the floor and coming back up in that rhythm. Move from the hip joint to avoid collapsing your chest. 6 1/2 Minutes.
    B. Continue bowing and rising up, but interlace your hands behind your back and, as you bow forward, lift your arms up as high as you can. Lower your arms as you rise back up. "You must learn to bow and you must learn your own strength." 7 Minutes.

Apply neck lock and raise head and shoulders 6" then raise feet up 6"

3. Lie down flat on your back.
    A. Apply neck lock and raise your head up six inches from the floor. Have your arms parallel to the floor palms down. Then also raise your feet six inches from the floor. Look at your toes and hold this position for 20 Seconds.
    B. From this position raise both your legs and your back up to sixty degrees, so that your body forms a "v" shape. Keep the arms parallel to the floor. Hold this position for 1 1/2 Minutes, then stay in the position and laugh for 1 Minute, then stop laughing and continue to hold the position for another 4 1/2 Minutes. (Position is held for a total of seven minutes.)

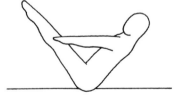

"Caliber will make you deliver. Character will sustain you. Consciousness will carry you. Courage will bring you honor. And commitment will bring you trust."
    YB

4. Come up into Half Wheel Pose. Once you are up and stable, begin Breath of Fire. 1 Minute.

5. Lie down and deeply relax for 7 Minutes. (Yogi Bhajan played the gong, instructing the students to project out in deep relaxation, leaving their bodies consciously and feeling as if they were flying above their body.)

Correct Nerve Shallowness

June 6, 1984

When the nervous system acts extraordinarily weak, the capability to be effectively calm and active becomes very shallow. It is not you who makes mistakes or who suffers. It is the nervous shallowness. Yogic science calls it 'slow wave contact.' The nervous authority, nervous center, nervous self is not effectively strong to communicate its own duties about the physical identity. Your physical identity has a frequency and your nervous center must correspondingly respond to it and when that is not coordinated well, the life is foggy. It is not clear. And mostly such life is based on emotional self, emotional extension, and emotional satisfaction. The problem with emotional satisfaction is, as much as you emotionally want to satisfy yourself, that shallow and empty you will feel. That's the problem. Because once you let the emotions rule you, there are millions of them. There is one consciousness and millions of emotions. Which one do you want to satisfy first? When? Where? When? Where? More! More! More! More! And that is what it is.

YB

"If you do not know what wisdom is, the only thing you will have is your neuroses."

1. Come into Half Wheel Pose. Do heavy-duty Breath of Fire through your mouth. 1 Minute. This exercise benefits the nervous system.

2. Stand up and bend forward, stretching your spine and bringing your head toward your knees. Keep your legs straight and interlace your hands behind your legs. Put your head through your legs if possible. Inhale through the mouth and exhale through the nose. Breathe quickly. 3 Minutes.

3. Come into Frog Pose. Move up and down quickly, doing Frog Pose exercise 108 times. Inhale through the mouth as you come up. Exhale through the mouth as you go down. (In the class, people counted their 108 Frogs out loud as they did them.)

4. Sit in Easy Pose. Fold your arms over your chest. Each hand grasps the upper portion of the opposite arm. Rotate your spine around your hips, moving heavy and fast. Move "as if you are grinding at the sides." 2 Minutes.

5. Lie down on your back with your hands on your chest. Inhale through your mouth and raise your torso, bending forward, bringing your forehead to your knees. Exhale through the nose and lie back down.
Continue 3 1/2 Minutes.

6. Still on your back. Inhale deeply and quickly (1-2 seconds) and exhale long and slow (12-15 seconds). Continue for 3 Minutes. (In class, Yogi Bhajan timed this breath with the beat of the gong, so to get the full benefit of this meditation, use the tape of this class for this portion of the set. This audio tape is available through Ancient Healing Ways as KYB 035.)

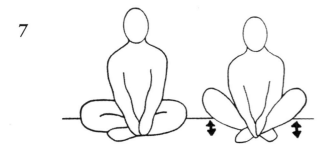

7. Briefly stretch and wiggle your body. Come sitting up in Easy Pose. Grab your front shin with both hands and bounce your knees up and down. Move fast and bounce the knees as high up and as far down as they can go. 1 1/2 Minutes.

8. In the same position as #7 (in Easy Pose, grasping your front shin with both hands), roll all the way back on your spine and return to a sitting position. Continue rolling back and forth for 1 Minute. (It's very relaxing if you do it right.)

25

Creating Magnetic Fields to Expand Your Inner Self

March 26, 1986

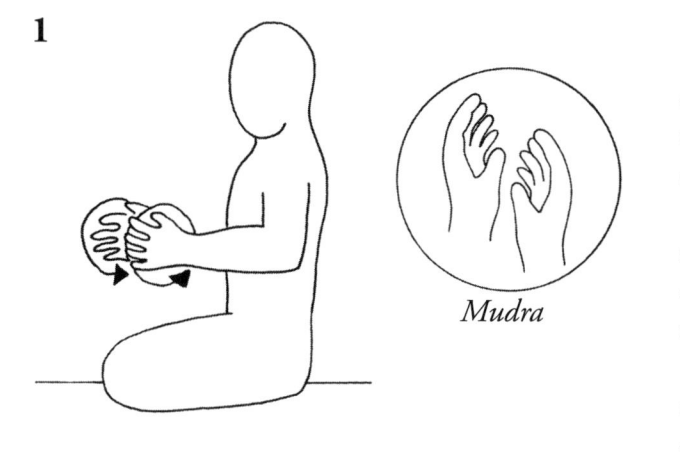

Mudra

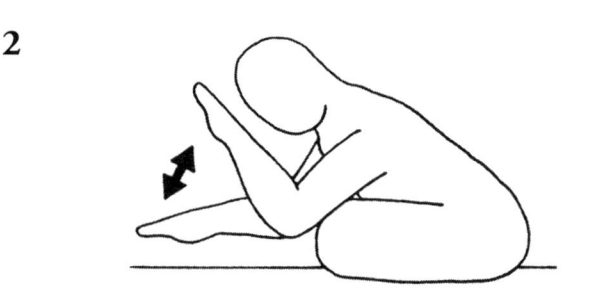

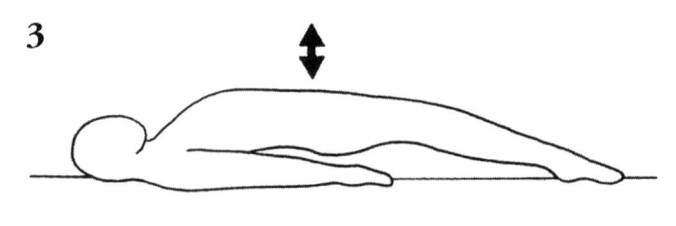

*The **Agn Granthi** is at the heart center. It is the place for the fire element of life: it circulates and purifies the blood and digests the food. It creates all the juices in us. When the energy here is not circulated properly, it can destroy us: it makes us angry, limited, intolerant, and uncommitted.*

Sometimes the most difficult thing for a person to do is to shift gears: shifting from anger or frustration to something more productive, moving the energy from one chakra to another. We are all built to be wise, intelligent, peaceful, and helpful. Why are our lives not that way?

In the West we feel that if we build our outside and expand ourselves materially, we will be strong and balance our lives, but this is wrong. There is an inner law that for every expansion, there is a corresponding contraction. You must work first to develop the spiritual power inside, then the power of the outside world will become smaller and you shall command.

1. Sit in Easy Pose. Bring your hands in front of your chest, with the fingers spread and slightly rounded. The hands are about six to eight inches apart, with the palms facing each other. Move the hands in circles, as if your hands are pedaling a bicycle. Move rapidly and feel a magnetic field being built between your two hands. Your hands will pick up their own magnetic identity, a vibratory magnetic field. 3 1/2 Minutes. Create a mental rage to fuel the movement, imagine your worst enemy and use that feeling.

2. Stay in Easy Pose and bend forward. Look at the floor and use your open hands to beat at it, but do not touch it. Once again you are using your hands to create a magnetic field. If you touch the floor you will lose the energy field you are creating. Move powerfully, using your anger, and you will find that this exercise will create a breath that cannot be achieved any other way. 2 Minutes. Sometimes your own magnetic field and the earth's magnetic field get out of sync, and that can make you very insecure.

3. Lie down flat on your back and pretend that you are lying on a "spinal-ator," one of those machines that you lie down upon and it flexes the spine from hips to shoulders. Vibrate and undulate your spine, bouncing your buttocks against the ground. 2 Minutes.

"Try this experiment: the next time that you become really angry, put your hand directly into some food and grab a handful. Eat it just like an animal. By the time you have finished eating the whole handful, your anger will be gone. It is a very physical thing. Anger from the heart gets into the mouth area, a distance of just about six inches."

YB

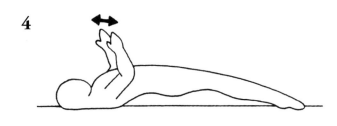

4. Lie down flat on your back, raise your hips up and make an arc of your body from heels to shoulders. Allow no bend in your knees. Using your shoulders as an anchor, begin rapidly clapping your hands as hard as you can without actually letting your hands touch. Move fast, keep the slant, and stretch the navel out. 1 1/2 Minutes. This position is hard to do, but it is soothing to the nerves.

5. Lie down flat on your back, place your palms against your face on either side of your nose. Begin massaging your face with circular motions of your hands, rubbing the sides of your nose in the process. Nose has to be massaged on the outside. While doing this massage, go to sleep. Hypnotize yourself. (In the class, Yogi Bhajan played the "Sat Nam, Wahe Guru #1 Indian Version" tape as he did a gong meditation.) 8 Minutes.

6. Plunge into a deep nap. Let your mind go into a deep sleep. Place your arms by your sides and deeply relax. 5 Minutes.

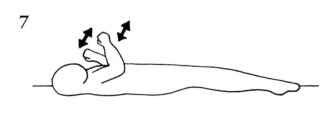

7. Still lying down, close your fists very tightly, and heavily pound at your heart center, "King Kong" style, but without actually touching your chest. This is a heavy, vigorous movement. 1 1/2 Minutes.

8. Still on your back, place your hands at your heart center, and totally relax. Chant with the cassette tape *Sat Nam Wahe Guru #1, Indian Version** and get lost in the heart center sound current of the chant. 3 1/2 Minutes.

*Sat Naam, Sat Naam, Jee
Sat Naam, Sat Naam, Jee
Wha Hay Guroo
Wha Hay Guroo
Wha Hay Guroo
Wha Hay Guroo

This set continues on page 27

9

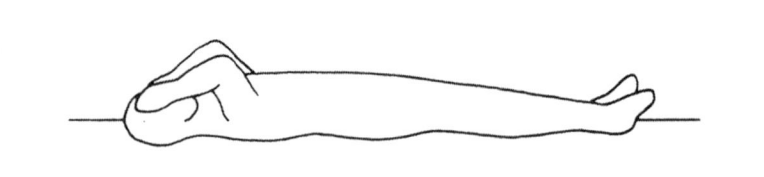

10

9. Place your hands on your forehead over your third eye point and chant along with Singh Kaur's tape of *Wahe Guru Jio*. 3 1/2 Minutes. Notice the difference between the music for this exercise and the last one. The previous chant was from the heart center and this one is from the third eye.

10. Place your hands over your navel point, concentrate there, and chant with the musical part of Liv Singh's *Har, Har, Mukande with Affirmations*. 3 Minutes. This chant is from the navel center, it has a different rhythm and effect.

11. Inhale, roll your hands and feet, and wake up.

Try to understand, through your experience, the difference in effect of the three different tapes played in exercises eight, nine, and ten. It will help you to understand how communication changes depending upon the chakra from which the communication is projected. (In chanting all three mantras, be sure to use the tip of the tongue to create the sound current.)

Experiencing the Relationship of the Pranic Body and the Physical Body

March 7, 1984

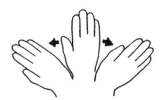

Keep the hand parallel to the floor.
Move it to the right.
Then back to center.
Move it to the left, then back to center.

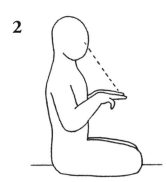

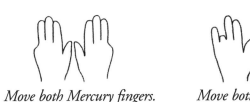

Move both Mercury fingers.   *Move both Sun fingers.*

Move both Saturn fingers.   *Move both Jupiter fingers.*

1. Sit in easy pose with the right elbow bent, forearm angled up, and the right palm facing downward. Concentrate on your right hand. Move it to the right to your maximum, then move it back to the center. Then move it to the left to your maximum and then back to the center. Keep the palm facing downward. 1 Minute.

Sometimes your hand will move in one direction a little bit more or less. The direction or the angle may be wrong. You will find that what you want to do is not happening. You will see that there is a difference between the command you send to your hand and its obedience. Observe this situation in this exercise.

2. Bend both elbows with the forearms angled up and both palms facing downward. The upper arms are relaxed by the sides of the body. The hands are together in front of the chest, thumbs near each other but not touching. Move both Mercury (pinkie) fingers down and up at the same time. Then move both Sun (ring) fingers down and up at the same time. Then move both Saturn (middle) fingers down and up at the same time. Then move both Jupiter (pointer) fingers down and up at the same time. Continue moving the same fingers of each hand at the same time. Move only the set of fingers that you are trying to move. Do not move any of the others. 2 1/2 Minutes.

Look at your hands, seriously concentrate, and coordinate the movement. Your efforts will show you that you have two brains, not one. Both movements will not be exactly the same, no matter what you do. This is a simple physical fact that is very hard to accept. We think that our hands are totally under our control and that they do what we tell them to do. You should be aware that everything is not under your control. It is not a handicap. It is a reality.

"What we are doing today is very important. We have one central nervous system. When that one central nervous system goes out of control, the re-entry of prana into the physical body is proportionately less. I want you to experience that. I want you to understand that the inflow of the pranic body and the physical body have an established relationship.

"Sometime you might have understood, in the simple sense of life, that a

29

3

3. Stand up, bend your knees, and lower yourself down as if you were sitting in a chair. Imagine that you are sitting comfortably in a chair. Stay in this position. Keep your back straight and your spine relaxed. 3 Minutes.

I am working with the organs of your body to let you know that because of the non-flexibility and rigidity which you have created, your functional body and your commanding body are not in the same position.
I want you to know this because this situation creates a handicap.

4. Sit down on your right heel with your left leg stretched out straight. Grasp the heel of your left foot with both hands and lift the leg up six inches. Lift it six inches only, no higher. Keep the left leg straight. Hold this position for 1 1/2 Minutes.
Remain in the posture, close your eyes, and do Sitali breath: inhale through the rolled tongue and exhale through the nose. Breathe heavily. 1 1/2 Minutes.
Change legs and continue the exercise sitting on the left heel, with the right leg stretched out in front. Grasp the right heel with both hands and lift the leg up six inches. Begin a powerful Breath of Fire. 2 Minutes.

4

In your body you have an organ called the colon. It gives you life. It gives you all that your body needs. If you can hold your leg straight and keep it in position for this exercise, you can help to strengthen your colon. This is one of many small cleansing kriyas that we do to affect certain important organs in our bodies.

On the left side we have done a cooling Sitali breath and on the right side we have done a heavy and hot Breath of Fire. Both must be done. Do not do one side and not the other. A couple of minutes of this breathing will trigger in you the strength that you cannot buy or capture.

5

5. Sit in Easy Pose and bring the soles of your feet together. Lock your hands around your feet, lift your feet off the ground, and balance yourself. It will be an angular balance. Do not let your feet touch the ground. Stick out your tongue as far as you can and begin panting dog breath. Make your breath deep and rhythmic. 1 1/2 Minutes.

This exercise is said to eliminate mucous and to take away sexual weakness.

person has died and after half an hour, they come back.
They are alive again. They say certain things, do certain things, and work out things for a couple of hours. Then they die again.
...It is just that the pranic body re-takes the life from the subtle body, pushes it back in (to the physical body), balances it out, and you are alive. Push it out and you are dead. That is the driving conclusion. We'll like to feel this relationship, so we may know about it.”

YB

6

6A

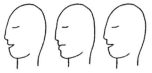

Open and close the lips.

6B

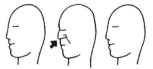

Wrinkle your nose up and down.

6C

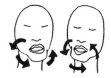

Roll the jaw.

7

6. Come into Cobra Pose.
   A. Begin rapidly opening and closing your lips. 1 1/2 Minutes. You will get a very funny feeling, but it is all right.
   B. Stay in Cobra Pose and begin wrinkling your nose. Pull your nose upward. 1 Minute. It is very relaxing. This exercise can get a tremendous amount of hate out of you. Get rid of it.
   C. Still in Cobra Pose, begin rolling your lower jaw, like a cow chewing its cud. The lower jaw moves around in a circle. This is a very relaxing movement. 1 Minute.

7. Sit in Easy Pose and stretch your arms out to the sides. Begin moving your arms up and down like you are flying. Imagine that you are flying a long distance. Close your eyes and concentrate on flying. 11 1/2 Minutes.

Fast or slow, set your own rhythm. Move in any pattern you wish, but whatever rhythm you start with, you have to continue in that rhythm. What we are doing is setting a movement and asking our neuro-message system to copy it. It is very important. You must recapture your original pattern and repeat it. It is all happening inside the brain and the movement of the hands is just a path to create it. It should not hurt.

To Finish: Stretch your arms straight to the sides like an eagle gliding. Make your arms and hands like steel. Toughen every muscle in your arms, shoulders, and neck. Stretch and toughen. 1 Minute.

8. Relax.

Eliminate Gastric and Heart Problems

June 19, 1984

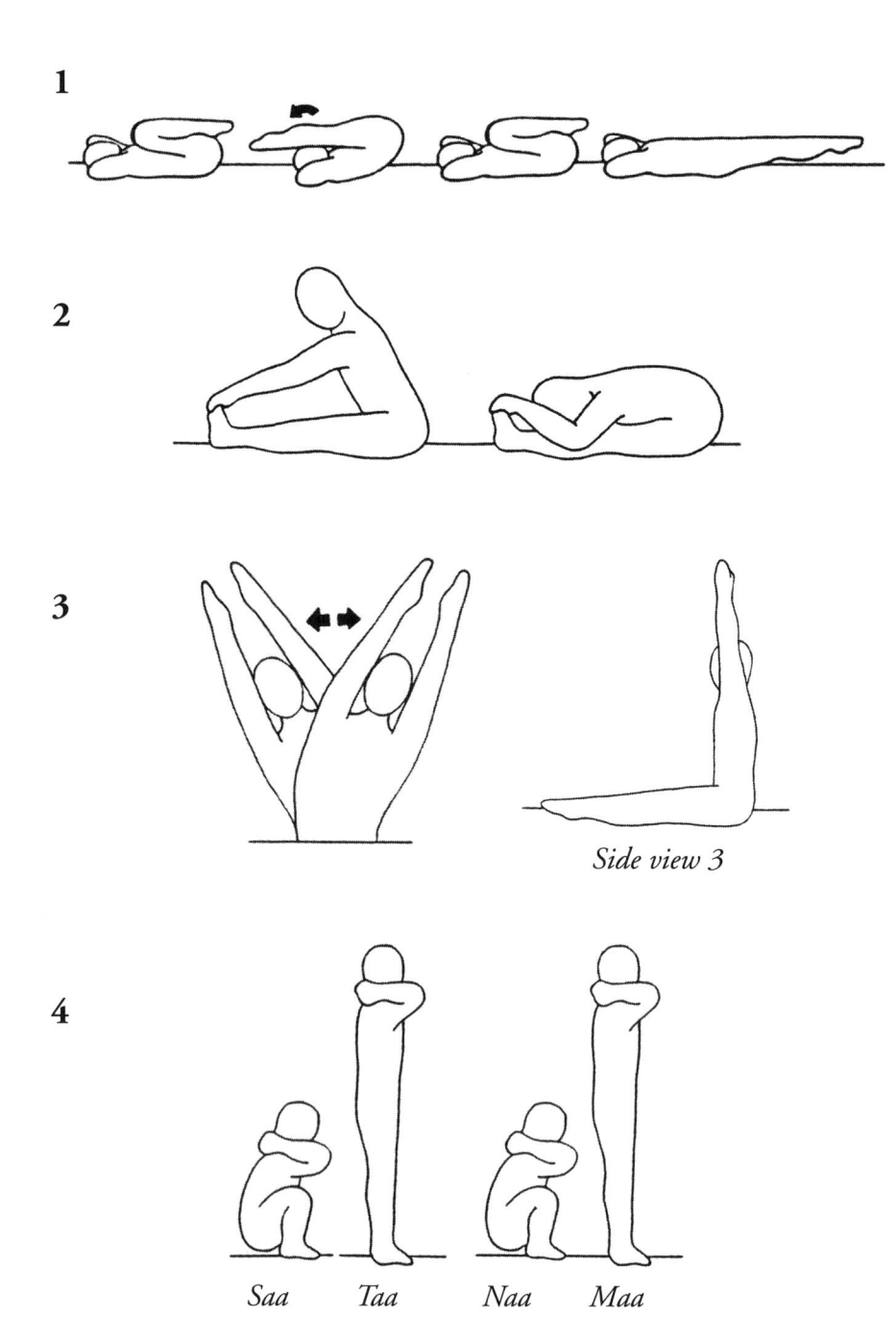

Side view 3

Saa   Taa   Naa   Maa

1. Lie down on your back and interlock your hands behind your head. Keep your legs straight and lift your heels off the floor. Then bring both of your knees to your chest. From this position bring your feet over your head so that your knees touch your nose. Return your knees to your chest and then stretch your legs out straight, keeping your heels off the floor. Continue this movement. Move quickly. The faster you do it, the better the effect. This exercise moves out old intestinal gas. 8 Minutes.

2. Sit up with your legs stretched out straight. Grab your toes and bend forward from your hips, bringing your nose to your knees. Then rise back up. Move up and down quickly to stimulate your circulation. Continue 3 Minutes.

3. Sit with your legs stretched out straight in front of you with your heels together. Raise your arms straight up with no bend in the elbows. Your palms face each other and your arms hug your ears. Begin bending from side to side, moving from the bottom of your rib cage to the tips of your fingers. Keep your palms the same distance apart throughout the movement. The upper body moves as one unit, like the trunk of a tree swaying in the wind. You are adjusting the rib cage. 2 Minutes.

4. Sit in Crow Pose with your hands interlocked behind your neck (touching the skin of your neck, under your hair). In this position, chant "Saa." Stand up and chant "Taa". Sit down in Crow Pose and chant "Naa." Stand up and chant "Maa." Bring a balance to your body by keeping your weight evenly distributed as you move up and down. Continue 4 1/2 Minutes.

"God rotates the earth and He is going to take care of your every routine. There is nothing to worry about."

YB

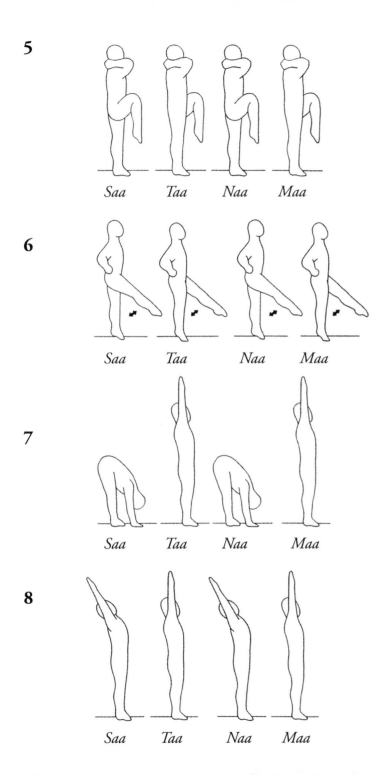

5. Stand up with your hands interlocked behind your neck. Chant "Saa" and bring your right knee up. Lower your right knee and lift the left knee as you chant "Taa."
Lower your left knee as you lift your right knee and chant "Naa". Raise your left knee and chant "Maa." Continue this sequence of movements for 1 Minute.

6. In a standing position, put your hands on your hips and alternately kick your legs forward. Move rapidly, scissoring your legs, and chanting "Saa -Taa-Naa-Maa" with the movement. This yogic kick dance lets the heart be stimulated. 3 Minutes.

7. In a standing position, raise your arms straight up over your head with your palms facing forward. Bend forward from your hips and touch the floor as you chant "Saa." Rise up with your hands over your head as you chant "Taa." Bend forward again and chant "Naa." Rise back up as you chant "Maa." Continue for 1 1/2 Minutes.

8. Still standing up with your hands straight up over your head, palms facing forward. Lift your chest and arch your body backward on "Saa." Return to standing straight on "Taa." Arch backward on "Naa." Straighten up on "Maa." 1 Minute. (Arch backward by lowering your shoulder blades and lifting your chest so that you create an arch with your whole back. Protect your lower back from compression as you arch backward by pulling in and up on your navel point to rotate your pelvis and elongate your lower back.)

9. Lie down, cover up, and deeply relax. 11-15 Minutes. (Yogi Bhajan played the gong for this meditative relaxation.)

Folding and Unfolding of the Energy
Working in the Third Chakra, the Navel Point

February 8, 1984

33

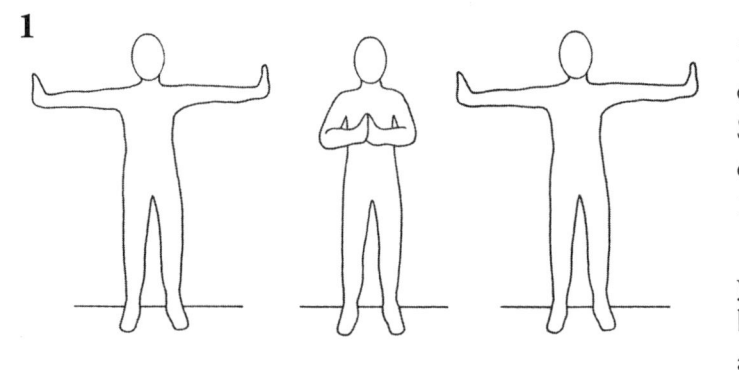

1. Stand straight with your feet a comfortable distance apart. Stretch your arms out to the sides, parallel to the floor, wrists bent, fingers pointing upward. Slowly and gracefully move your hands from this position to Prayer Pose at the center of your chest and then return your hands back to the starting position. 1 Minute.

Continue moving your hands this way and pull in on the navel point when your hands are in Prayer Pose. Release the navel pull when your hands stretch back out to the sides. Move slowly and systematically. Your breath will automatically adjust to the movement. Continue 2 1/2 Minutes.

2. Stand straight with your feet a comfortable distance apart. Stretch your arms out to the sides, parallel to the floor, wrists bent, fingers pointing upward. Keep your spine straight as you bend to the left side, come back to the center, and then bend to the right side and come back to the center. Continue 3 1/2 Minutes.

3. Stand straight with your arms stretched straight out in front of you. Lower your body into a squatting position in eight movements while counting the movements out loud. Move deeper into the squat with each count. At the count of "one" you are standing straight up and at the count of "eight" you are in Crow Pose. Then rise back up in one motion and begin the count again. 3 Minutes.

"Education is not what you learn from time. Education is what you learn from your intuition and apply to time."

YB

One　　*Two*　　*Three*　　*Four*　　*Five*　　*Six*　　*Seven*　　*Eight*

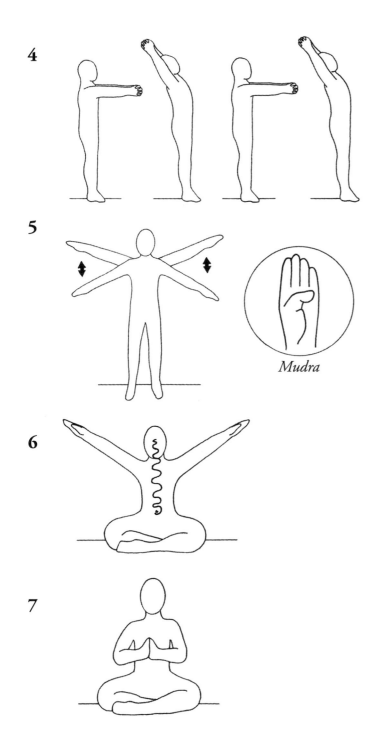

4. Stand straight, interlace your fingers, and stretch your arms out in front of you. Keep the elbows straight. Lift your chest, and arch backward as you raise your arms up over your head. Return to the starting position. Continue this movement for 1 Minute.

5. Stand straight with your arms stretched out to the sides, palms down. Move your arms up and down as if you are flying. Move quickly. 1 1/2 Minutes.

Touch your thumbs to the Mound of Mercury (the mound at the base of the little finger) and continue moving your arms up and down with your hands in this mudra. 1 1/2 Minutes.

6. Sit down in Easy Pose with your arms up and spread in an open "v". Tilt your palms forward at a sixty-degree angle. (The palms are neither facing straight forward nor facing downward. They are angled in between, at sixty degrees.) Hold this position and meditate. Mentally chant any mantra you choose as you gently pump your navel point. Use the navel to vibrate your mantra from your navel up to your third eye. 2 1/2 Minutes.

7. Bring your hands into Prayer Pose and chant "Sat Naam" in the *long Sat Naam* form. (Sat is chanted for either 8 or 35 beats and Naam is chanted for one beat.) 8 Minutes.
(Yogi Bhajan gave an alternate body position for this meditation: each hand clasps the opposite forearm below the elbow. The arms may be either against the body or held out at shoulder height.)

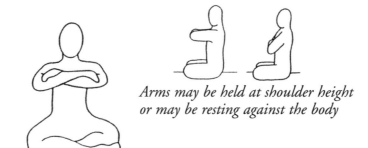

Arms may be held at shoulder height or may be resting against the body

#7 Alternative position

8

8. Still in Easy Pose, clap your hands in front of your chest as you chant "Sat" and move your arms out to the sides, parallel to the ground, with the elbows straight and the palms facing forward as you chant "Naam." 2 1/2 Minutes.

9. Relax.

These are simple exercises that stimulate the psyche, the sciatic nerve, the energy, and the main meridian in the brain (the vagus nerve). You have only to follow the directions for the set. Slowly and gradually extend the length of practice time for each exercise to 5-7 minutes. You will feel light. It will make you feel good.

Kriya For Achieving Comfortable, Happy Sleep

May 9, 1984

1

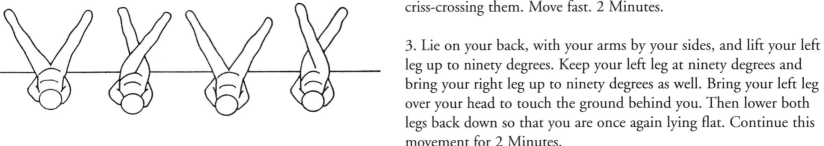

1. Lie on your back with your legs stretched out straight and your body relaxed. Raise the left arm up to ninety degrees and the right leg up to ninety degrees. Hold this position while you raise and lower your head as fast as you can. This is called "hammering the head." 1 1/2 Minutes.

2. Still on your back, place both hands under your lower back for support, lift both legs up, and rapidly move them side to side, criss-crossing them. Move fast. 2 Minutes.

3. Lie on your back, with your arms by your sides, and lift your left leg up to ninety degrees. Keep your left leg at ninety degrees and bring your right leg up to ninety degrees as well. Bring your left leg over your head to touch the ground behind you. Then lower both legs back down so that you are once again lying flat. Continue this movement for 2 Minutes.

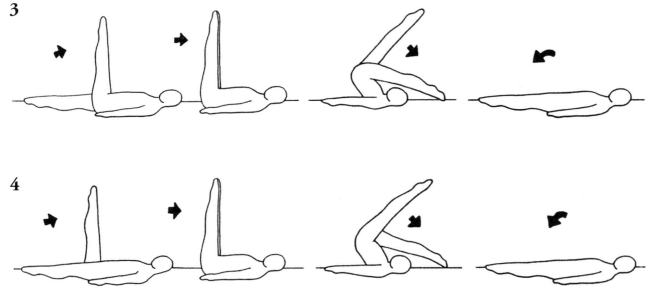

4. Repeat exercise #3, but change the leg that touches the ground behind you. In this exercise bring the right leg up to ninety degrees and then bring the left leg up to ninety degrees. Bring the right leg over to touch the ground behind the head. Then lower both legs back down so that you are once again lying flat. 2 Minutes.

"The best love is to serve all equally."
    YB

5

5. Sit in Easy Pose and lock your hands behind your lower back. Bend forward, touching your forehead to the floor, and raising your arms up behind you into Yoga Mudra. Sit back up straight as you lower your arms. Continue bowing and rising up. Move quickly. 2 Minutes.

6

6. Come onto your hands and knees and begin Cat-Cow. Move quickly. 1 Minute.

7

7. Sit in Crow Pose and lock your hands on top of your head. Inhale and rise up to standing, exhale and squat back into Crow Pose. Maintain your balance with your elbows. Continue 1 Minute. Move fast. (This exercise shows whether your electro-magnetic field is in shape.)

8

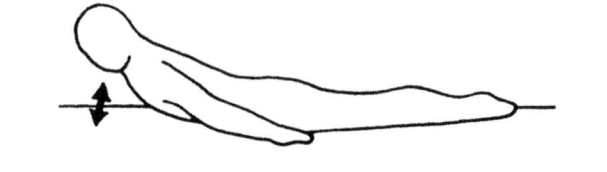

8. Lie on your stomach with your arms by your sides. Use your navel to press your hips into the floor and raise your chest up off the floor without using your hands. Pull the shoulder blades away from your ears to help lift the chest. Move quickly up and down. This exercise adjusts the ribs if you can do it correctly and quickly. 1 Minute.

9A

9B

10

11

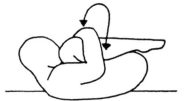

12

9. Lie on your stomach.
   A. Reach back and grab your left leg with both hands. Raise and lower your chest while holding onto your left leg. Move fast for 20 Seconds.
   B. Change legs and repeat the movement for 20 Seconds while holding the right leg with both hands. Move fast.

10. Come into Cobra Pose and then lower yourself back down to the ground. Continue lifting up into Cobra and lowering the chest back to the ground. Move fast and feel free. 20 Seconds.

11. Quickly, lie on your back, lock your arms around your knees and bring your nose to your knees. Roll from side to side. (The roll is from left to right, not from head to hips.) 1 1/2 Minutes.

12. Lie down flat on your stomach with your arms by your sides, palms facing up. Go to sleep for 31 to 45 Minutes. This sleep time is a required part of this set.

   This set works to stimulate the navel point area so that we can experience *Sukh Nidra*, which is comfortable happy sleep. Ideally, if you do these exercises before bed and then go to sleep for the night, it will take away weird dreams and give you wonderful subconscious clearance.

Move the Glandular System

May 30, 1984
Evening Class

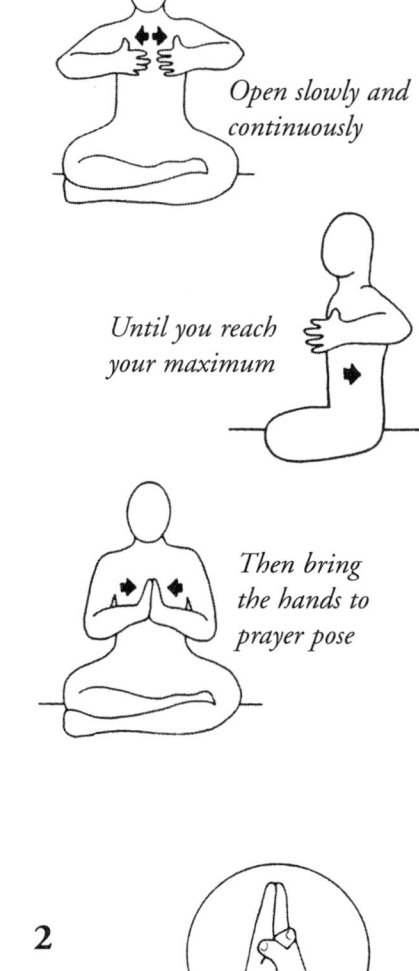

Open slowly and continuously

Until you reach your maximum

Then bring the hands to prayer pose

1. Sit in Easy Pose with the elbows bent, forearms parallel to the floor, and the palms facing the chest. The fingers are held open and moderately stiff. The hands are about two inches from each other and four to six inches from the chest. From this position, very slowly pull the arms apart, moving with tension, until the arms are alongside the ribs with the fingers pointing straight forward. This movement is very slow and very tight. You are opening up your chest and you must open to your own individual capacity. Move at one slow consistent speed and with mechanical accuracy. (The pull open should take about thirty seconds.) When you have opened up to your maximum, quickly bring the hands together in prayer pose in front of your chest. Move fast. Then return to the starting position and begin the movement again. 3-7 Minutes.

When you are sick, only a part of you is sick, not your totality. If, in this exercise you feel a place where your movement becomes jerky or speeds up, it shows that your movement has not got the necessary consistency and your general magnetic field, the basic strength of your life, is weak in some area. This exercise can correct that weakness if, the next time you reach the area where your movement became jerky, you maintain your speed and consistency. Magnetic power corrects the magnetic field and magnetic power is nothing but your own movement. Do it oriental style by concentrating on it. Make your movement totally smooth and continuous.

2. Put your hands together in Prayer Pose and cross your thumbs to lock them together. Maintain this mudra throughout the exercise. Count the movements out loud and establish a steady even rhythm.

    One: push your arms up to the right at a sixty-degree angle across your body and at a sixty- degree angle up. Your arms will be pointing to the right, elbows straight. Bring your hands back to the center of your chest.

    Two: push your arms up to the left at a sixty-degree angle across your body and at a sixty-degree angle up. Your arms will be pointing to the left, elbows straight. Then bring your hands back to the center of your chest.

Mudra

One	Two	Three	Four	
Right and back to center	*Left and back to center*	*Stay at center*	*Up and back to center*	*Angle of arm position #4*

"Kundalini Yoga started when all the sages and wisemen understood that there has to be a human life, a householder's life, a 'gristi.' Gristi means one who has an acknowledged control on self. Then the sages thought, 'We cannot teach them all this yoga which takes years and years. Where is the time for marriage, family, and earning a living?' So they decided to come out with a

3

Three: stay still with your hands in prayer pose at the center of your chest.

Four: bring your arms up to the front at a sixty-degree angle. Then bring your hands back to the center of your chest. Begin again at "One". Move continuously through the positions at the count for 3 Minutes.

Now continue the movement, adding a mantra, and moving very slowly with tension in the hands. Chant "Saa" as your arms move to the right. "Taa" as your arms move to the left. "Naa" as you stay still with your hands in front of your chest. "Maa" as your arms move up to the front. 3 Minutes.

4 & 6

3. Place your hands over the center of your chest, fingers overlapping, thumbs against your chest and pointing upward. Twist left and right, moving the upper body as one unit. Chant "Saa" and twist to the left. Chant "Taa" when you return to center. Chant "Naa" as you twist to the right and chant "Maa" as you come back to center. Continue twisting and chanting 2 1/2 Minutes.

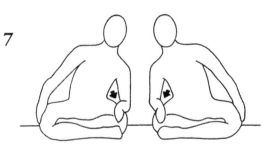

4. Come into Front Platform Pose, with the body in a straight line from head to heels. Hold yourself steady in the position for 1 Minute and then, for the next 30 Seconds, think about all the people that you are mad at. Use that anger as fuel and begin alternate leg lifts while maintaining Front Platform. 4 1/2 Minutes. The ideal pace is one leg lifted every two seconds. *This exercise can get rid of the extra hidden anger of centuries that you brought in to this life from previous incarnations.*

7

5. Sit down in Easy Pose and relax for 1 Minute.

6. Repeat Exercise #4 for 7 Minutes. This exercise works on the thighbone area, which is responsible for regulating the calcium/magnesium balance in your blood. The balance of these minerals affects your mental balance.

8

7. Sit down in Easy Pose with your hands on your knees. Bend to the left side, bending between the diaphragm and the hipbone. Don't bend any other part of your body. Then bend to the right side. Continue alternately bending to each side. This is a slouchy bend. The bottom of the ribs, on the bending side, moves toward the hipbone, giving your side a comfortable squeeze. This movement can stimulate and cleanse the kidneys. 1 1/2 Minutes.

8. Put your hands in your lap, right hand resting in the left, palms upward, thumbs touching. Inhale deeply and exhale deeply three times. Then inhale deeply and hold your breath for 20-30 seconds. Repeat this breath sequence two more times and then relax.

science which, in a couple of minutes, can put you together and keep you going. A science to create a glandular secretion that keeps the standard of life in a spirit high enough so that the consumption of energy in a householder's day is equal to the energy he can produce in a couple of minutes doing Kundalini Yoga."

YB

41

1

Moving the
right hand

Moving the
left hand

2

3

Up   Flat   Down

4

Start position   Lean back and come forward

Refreshing the Nervous System

February 15, 1984

1. Sit in Easy Pose with your spine straight. Lift the chest up and out and pull the chin in. Extend your arms out to the sides parallel to the floor with the elbows straight. Bend both wrists so that your fingers point upward. Circle the right hand around its wrist, moving the hand and fingers only. Move the hand in an inward circle keeping the elbow straight. Move carefully, grabbing the space with the hand and pulling it toward you. Pull the energy out, pull the space inward. Use the wrist, the hand, the palm, and the fingers, but not the arm. Move the energy very silently and effectively. Keep the left hand straight and still, with the fingers pointing upward. Keep the left arm very straight, no bend in the elbow.
This exercise can make you mentally very itchy, because you are moving an area that you don't usually move. 7 Minutes.

Change sides and move your left hand in an inward circle. Keep your right arm extended straight out to the side and keep the right hand still, with the fingers pointing upward. 2 1/2 Minutes.

Keep the angle right. It is the angle of the one hand and the movement of the other hand that creates a co-relationship within your energy field. This exercise affects the thyroid and parathyroid very powerfully. You may have to cough.

2. Stay in Easy Pose and clap your hands vigorously. 15-20 Seconds.

3. Sit straight with your chin in and chest out. Stretch your arms straight out in front of you, parallel to the floor, with the palms facing down. The hands are about 9" apart. Moving both hands together: bend the hands up at the wrist and bring them back to the palms flat position; then bend the hands down at the wrist and bring them back to up position and begin the sequence again. This is a three-part movement: up, flat, down. And then up again. Use a forceful, jerky movement. Sometimes it will feel soothing and sometimes it will feel annoying. 3 1/2 Minutes.

4. Sit with in Easy Pose with your spine straight and stretch your arms out to the sides for balance (like wings). The palms face forward. Lean back slightly, keeping your spine straight and moving your arms and upper body as one unit. Come back upright and continue this movement. This is a movement of the hip

"Working by heart means using your feelings and emotions to lead you to your spiritual sense of existence."

YB

5

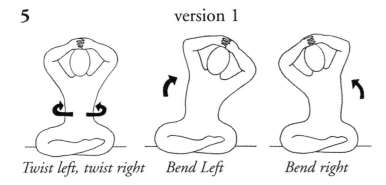

version 1

Twist left, twist right *Bend Left* *Bend right*

version 2

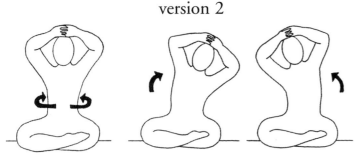

Then bend left and right 15 times *Twist left and right 15 times*

6

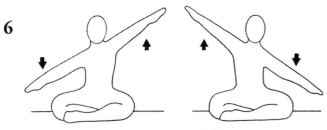

Arms move up and down...

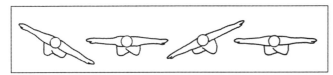

as the shoulders twist forward and back.

joint. Lean back to the maximum point you can, where you feel like you are going to tip over, but keep your legs on the floor. This is the point where the exercise does its work. It builds muscle tone in that area where people sometimes get hernias. Meditate, say, "Bless me, God," and lean back with devotion. 6 1/2 Minutes.

5. For exercise #5, you may *either* do Version #1 or Version #2. **Do not do both versions.** Whichever version you choose, that version is to be done for a maximum of 7 Minutes.

Version #1: Sit in Easy Pose and interlace your fingers on top of your head. Move rapidly through the following sequence, moving your torso as one unit:
  A. Twist to the left.
  B. Twist to the right.
  C. Bend to the left side.
  D. Bend to the right side and then begin the sequence again at "A".

Version #2: Sit in Easy Pose and interlace your fingers on top of your head. Twist left and right fifteen times. (One twist left and one twist right counts as "one time.") Then bend to the left side and to the right side fifteen times. (One bend left and one bend right counts as "one time.") Continue alternately doing fifteen twists and then fifteen bends.

6. Stretch your arms out to the sides with your palms facing down. Keep your arms in a straight line through your shoulders like airplane wings. Move the left arm up sixty degrees as the right arm moves down sixty degrees. Move the right arm up to sixty degrees as the left arm moves down sixty degrees. Move slowly and rhythmically. Then add another element to the movement. As your arms are moving up and down, begin twisting left and right to angle the arms forward and back.

Your arms will be moving up and down and at the same time the whole upper body is twisting from side to side. 2 1/2 Minutes. *It is a hard movement, but if you do it rhythmically, you can cover yourself.*

7

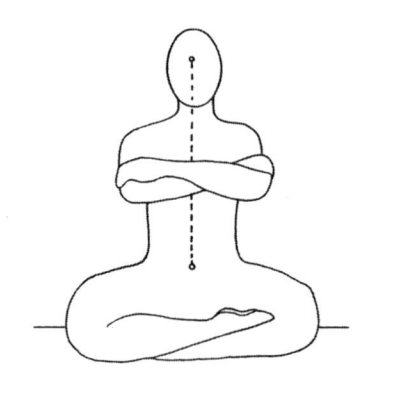

7. Sit with your arms folded over your chest, right arm over left. Chant "Har Haray" in a monotone. The pace is one "Har Haray" per second. Concentrate at the third eye point. Pull the energy from the navel up to the third eye point. Move the energy. 5 Minutes.

8. Sit on your heels and bend forward into Baby Pose. Rest your forehead on the floor and your arms on the floor by your sides.
2 Minutes.
   This position is good to do every day because it creates an inflow of spinal serum that refreshes the nerves of the spinal column.

8

9. Stand on your knees with your hands interlaced behind your neck. Press your knees into the floor and lift your chest arching your spine backward. Bend as far back as you can without losing your balance. 2 Minutes.
   This is the opposite of Baby Pose. Think elevated thoughts in this posture, feeling yourself to be mentally neutral. Don't feel very wise, don't feel very foolish, just feel to BE.

10. Relax.

9

Work on the Meridians

May 30, 1984
Morning Class

One   Two   Three & Four

1. Sit in Easy Pose with your palms together in front of your chest.
    One: stretch your arms straight out to the sides, parallel to the ground, with the wrists bent and the fingers pointing upward. Your palms face outward.
    Two: bring your palms together over your head with your elbows straight.
    Three: bring your arms down so that your palms are together in front of the center of your chest, but not touching it.
    Four: stay in position three. This is the non-active command, also called the "non-committing action."
Repeat this sequence for 3 Minutes. Move quickly.

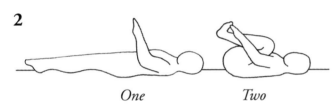

One   Two

2. Lie on your back.
    One: lie flat on your back with your forearms up so that your palms face your feet.
    Two: bend your knees and bring your feet up to touch your hands.
    (At the next count of "one" return to lying flat on your back with your forearms up so that your palms face your feet.)
Repeat this sequence for 3 Minutes. Move quickly so that movements one and two are completed in two seconds. (There should be no noise when your heels return to the ground.)

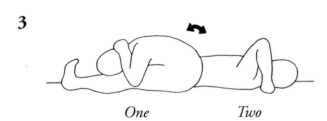

One   Two

3. Remain on your back, interlace your fingers, and place them behind your neck so that they touch the skin. Move from position to position at the count:
    One: sit up and bring your head to your knees.
    Two: lie back down.
Repeat this sequence for 3 1/2 Minutes. Movements one and two should be completed in four seconds. This exercise is beneficial to the liver and digestive tract.

4. Come on to your hands and knees and do Cat Cow to loosen up your shoulders and keep them from getting locked. Move quickly. 30 Seconds. The lower back and shoulders must move.

"When your understanding is 'I belong to God and God belongs to me'; when that equation is complete, you are a saint. Then everything will come to you. You don't have to hustle."
YB

Warm up for #5

5

One   Two   Three   Four

6

One   Two

7

One   Two   Three   Four

8

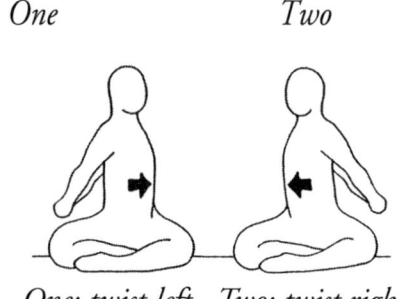

One: twist left   Two: twist right

5. Come into Back Platform Pose. Keep your body in one straight line. Your hands and feet are flat on the floor. Your fingers point toward your feet. Stay in Back Platform and raise and lower your left leg for 15 seconds. Then begin alternate leg lifts. Move from position to position at the count:

    One: lift your left leg up to ninety degrees.
    Two: lower your left leg.
    Three: lift your right leg up to ninety degrees
    Four: lower your right leg.

Continue this sequence for 1 Minute. Movements one through four should be completed in four seconds. Speed up for the last ten seconds.

6. Sit in easy pose with your hands behind your back, fingers interlocked. Move from position to position at the count:

    One: bend forward, raising your arms up as high as possible while bringing your forehead to the floor.
    Two: come sitting up straight.

Continue for 30 Seconds.

7. Come into Cobra Pose and move at the count.

    One: stay in Cobra Pose and touch your buttocks with your left hand.
    Two: return your left hand to the floor and touch your buttocks with your right hand.
    Three: return your right hand to the floor and touch your buttocks with your left hand.
    Four: return your left hand to the floor and touch your buttocks with your right hand.

Continue for 2 Minutes, speeding up the movement after the first minute. For the first minute, movements one through four are completed in four seconds. For the second minute, movements one through four are completed in two seconds.

Then lie down on your stomach with your head turned to one side and relax for thirty seconds.

8. Sit in Easy Pose and interlace your fingers behind your back. Stretch your arms away from your shoulders and lift them up as high as you comfortably can. Move at the count.

    One: twist to the left
    Two: twist to the right.

Twisting both left and right is completed in two seconds. Swing forcefully. This powerful swing can keep your heart healthy. Continue 2 1/2 Minutes.

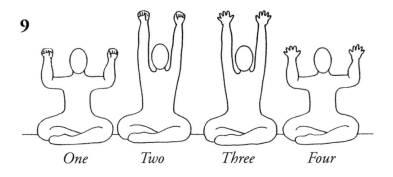

9. Sit in easy pose and move at the count.
   One: your arms are bent at the elbows, keeping your upper arms parallel to the floor. Your hands are in fists.
   Two: keep your hands in fists and raise your arms straight up.
   Three: keep the arms up but open the hands.
   Four: keep the hands open but bend the elbows so the arms are in the same position as "One." Continue for 1 1/2 Minutes.
Movements one through four are completed in three to four seconds.

10. Sit in Easy Pose with your arms out to the sides, elbows straight and palms down. Move one arm up as the other arm moves down. Keep your arms in one straight line. The trunk of the body should sway with this movement. Chant "Har" in a whisper each time one of your arms moves down. The movement is paced so that the chanting is continuous. Rhythm and energy are important. After 4 1/2 Minutes begin to chant out loud for 1 Minute more.

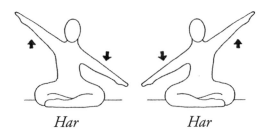

11. Lie down on your back and relax. 10 Minutes. In this recorded class, Yogi Bhajan played the gong to take the students into the "bio-rhythm of the left initial brainwaves."

It is highly recommended that you obtain the audiotape for this class so that you may experience Yogi Bhajan directing the exercises. It is virtually impossible to understand how the exercises are timed without his expert guidance. This tape (KYB 029) is available from Ancient Healing Ways (see page II). When this class was taught, Yogi Bhajan himself counted out the exercises. In exercise one he playfully mixed up the count, which confused the movement of the students. He wanted the students to be alert and use their brains to control the movement.

"We have an initial habit to obey…What we should obey and what we should not obey—that is what we have to learn. That deciding factor is the left side of the brain. Not the right side. In life if your left side is not effectively, initially, creatively, projectively active, the right side will commit so many mistakes that you can't even calculate it. Essentially, initially, you must remember that you are you…Otherwise everything else you do is without a base. It does not have a foundation."

Yogi Bhajan explained, "You get angry, you fight, and you get argumentative to the extent that you become obnoxious. For which you have to apologize and you have to be sorry. Because your right initiator is okay, it can project out the anger so that you become destructive. This can occur because your left initiator is not coordinating. Having the left initiator of the brain not coordinating makes you incomplete. You will be only one-third of a person, doesn't matter what religion you belong to or what country you belong to."

In one exercise, when the students continued with the original movement even though he called a different sequence of numbers, Yogi Bhajan said, "Things become routine. Life becomes routine. If anything is out of routine, you fall apart…It is as simple as that. (Not being able to follow the count as given) shows how our patterns are set and how we become 'not-conscious'. You have to understand what makes you 'not-

Ribcage, Lungs, and Lymphatic System

January 27, 1986

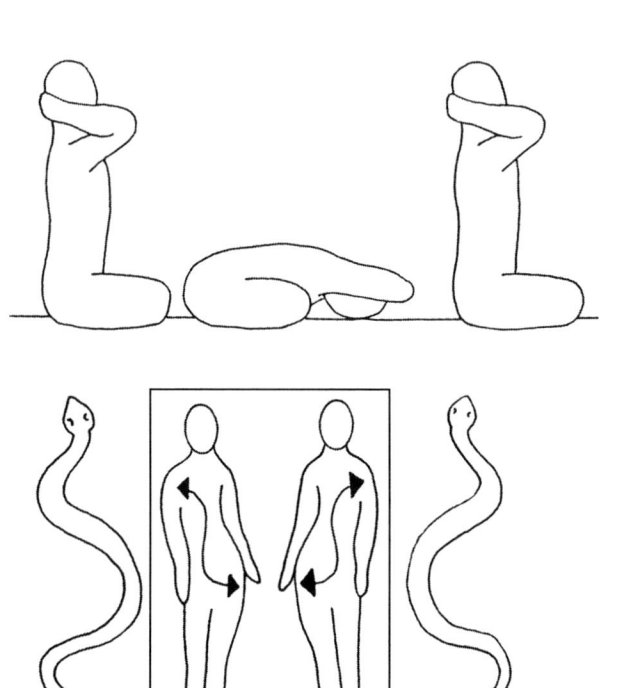

Let us see how our ribcage is held and how it is associated with the rest of the body.

1. Sit in Easy Pose and interlock your hands behind your head. Bend forward from your hips, bowing and bringing your forehead to the floor. Then rise back up. Continue this movement, moving slowly and gracefully. Inhale deeply and bend forward. Exhale completely as you rise back up. Breathe powerfully. Make 52 bows.

This exercise stimulates the lymphatic system, the protective system of the body. It also works on the hip joint. Rarely do we do this kind of movement in our daily lives. The hips are the cause of many troubles because in many cases, they are not getting the exercise they need.

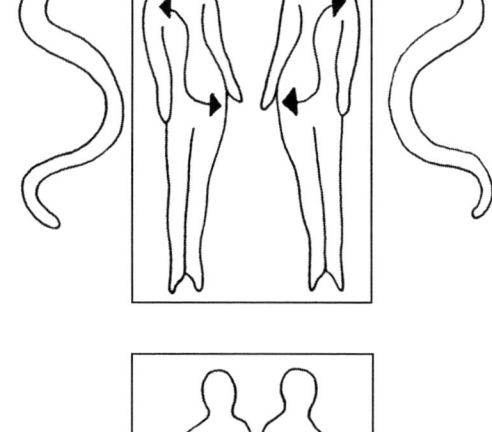

2. Lie down on your back with your legs stretched out straight. Move from side to side like a snake crawling through the grass. Move from your feet and ankles up to your hips, waist, and shoulders. When this movement is done with a powerful breath, it stimulates and strengthens the lymphatic system. Move powerfully, don't slow down. 3 Minutes.

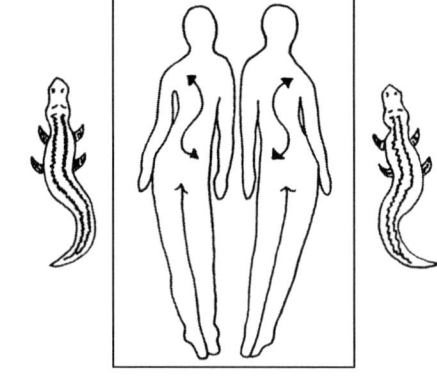

3. Turn onto your stomach and continue the same side to side, whole body movement. Pretend that you are a big crocodile, strong and mighty, slithering along a riverbank. Move with rhythm and strength to give the lymph glands a natural strengthening and bring benefit to your spine and your digestion. 3 1/2 Minutes.

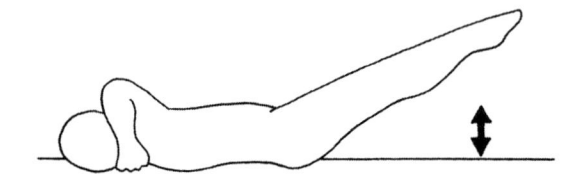

4. Lie on your back with your hands under your neck. Keep your legs together. Inhale as you raise your legs, bringing your heels up two feet from the floor. Exhale as you lower your legs back to the floor. 4 Minutes.

"Consult your spirit, your soul, on everything."

YB

5

6

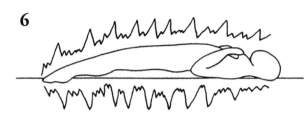

7

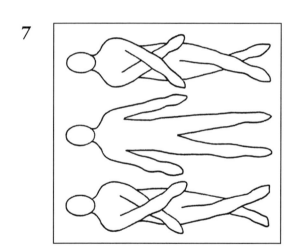

9

5. Remain lying on your back and raise your arms up to ninety degrees. Make your hands into fists. Inhale heavily as you bring your hands toward your chest. Move with great tension, as if you were pulling a heavy weight toward your chest. Exhale as you raise your fists back up to ninety degrees. Once your arms are straight up, open your fists. Make your hands back into fists and inhale as you again bring your fists toward your chest. Continue 3 1/2 Minutes.

6. Still lying on your back, place the palms of your hands on the center of your chest. Begin to jump your body around like a "fish in a frying pan." If you do this movement as a meditative act, you can achieve a hydro balance in your body. 1 1/2 Minutes.

7. Still lying on your back, raise your arms and legs up off the ground. Begin criss-crossing your arms and legs (moving from side to side, not up and down). Breathe powerfully. 2 1/2 Minutes.

8. Lie on your back and deeply nap. 5 1/2 Minutes. Gently return to an active state by rolling your hands and feet and doing a few cat stretches. Then rise up into a sitting position.

9. Sit in Easy Pose with your spine straight. Put your hands together at the center of your chest to pray for tranquility and peace within you and for the universe. Sit calmly and gently, in absolute peace and tranquility. Chant with Livtar Singh Khalsa's recording of *I Am Thine, in Mine, Myself*:

> Hummee, Humm, Toommee Toom, Wah Hay Guroo
> I am Thine, in mine, myself. Wah Hay Guroo.

Chant out loud for 6 Minutes. Then chant mentally and silently, connecting the inner chant with the Universal Mind. 1 Minute.

Then inhale and hold your breath for 30 Seconds as you pray for peace within yourself and throughout the world. Pray on this breath, which you have held. Exhale and relax.

Working the Command Post Area

June 13, 1984

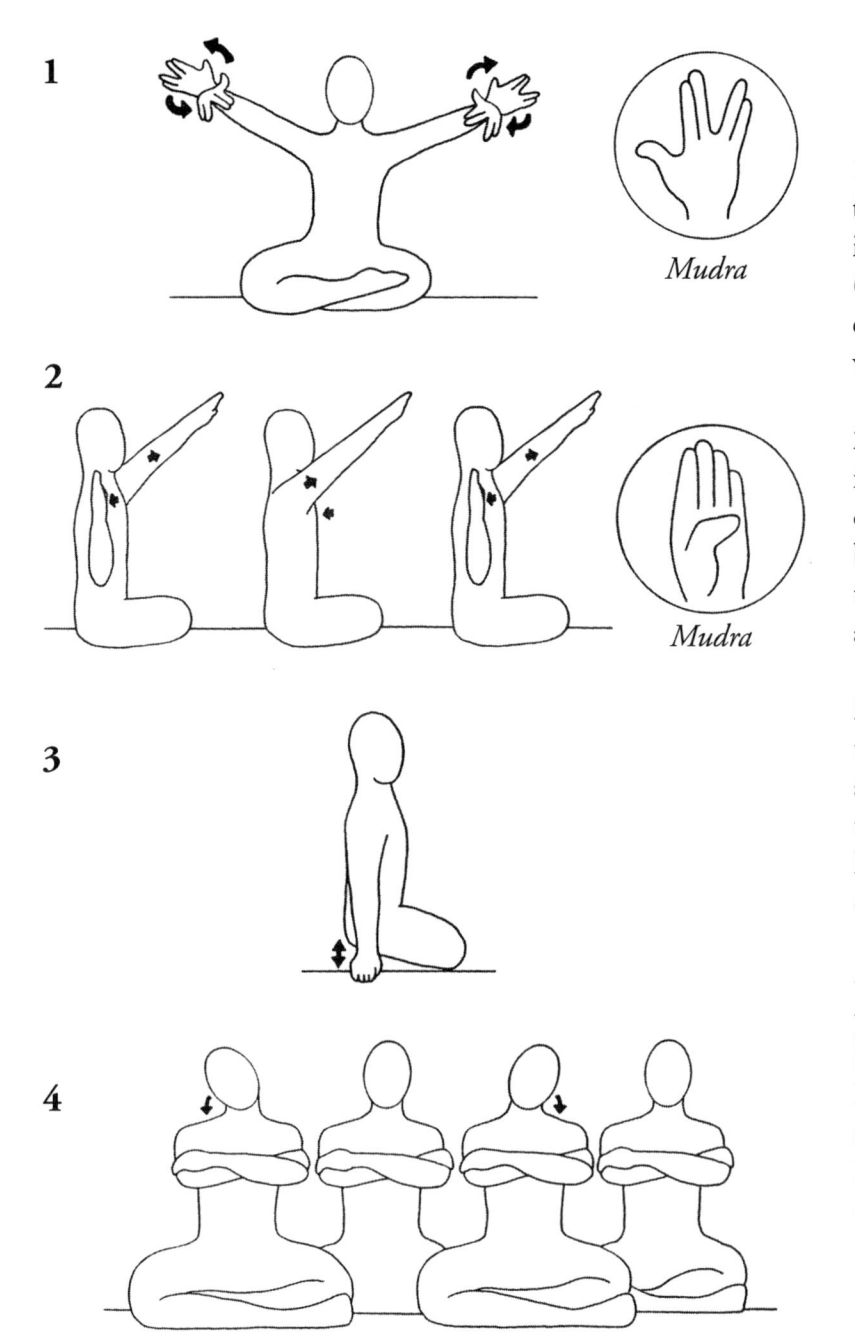

Mudra

Mudra

1. Sit in Easy Pose with your arms stretched up and angled out to the sides (No exact angle was specified.) Start with your palms facing downward. Split your fingers to create a "V" between your Saturn (middle) and Sun (ring) fingers. Keep your arms in position with your elbows straight and your fingers split as you rotate your hands on your wrists. Keep moving, do not slow down at all. 4 1/2 Minutes.

2. Sit in Easy Pose with your arms bent at the elbows, palms facing forward at shoulder level. Place each thumb on the mound at the base of the Mercury (little) finger. Extend your left arm up and out and bring it back to the starting position. As the left arm returns, extend the right arm up and out. Continue this movement, making it a quick action. Move fast. 1 1/2 Minutes.

3. Sit in Easy Pose and make your hands into fists. Place your fists on the ground on either side of your hips. Begin body drops, pushing against the floor with your fists to raise yourself up and then releasing the push so that your body drops back down. Move fast like a jackhammer. Yogi Bhajan called this a "jovial exercise" and told the students to be energetic in doing it. 3 Minutes.

4. Fold your arms in front of your chest at shoulder level. Start with your head up straight. Then bend your head to the left, bringing your left ear toward your left shoulder. Then bring your head straight. Bend your head to the right, bringing your right ear toward your right shoulder. Bring your head straight up. Continue this movement 1 1/2 Minutes. (Yogi Bhajan set a pace of 4 seconds for the entire sequence of movements: bend left, up straight, bend right, and up straight.)

"Free will is essential for existence, but also that free will should listen to your inner will. People have been told there is a 'God's will'. When you say that, it looks like God's will is outside of you. That is not true. There is no such thing as God's will outside of you. There is a God's will inside of you."

YB

5

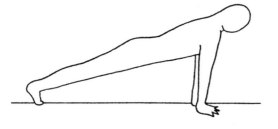

6

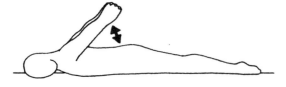

7A

7B

Har   Har   Har   Har

5. Lie down on your stomach. Put your hands under your shoulders and rise up into Front Platform Pose, with the body in one straight line from head to heels. Keep your body straight and still. Turn off your thoughts. *If you can stop thinking, you can totally stop worrying. That's the purpose.* 3 Minutes.

6. Lie down flat on your stomach. Interlock your fingers at the base of your spine. Raise your hands up into Yoga Mudra and lower them back down. Breathe powerfully and move fast. 4 Minutes.

7. Sit in Easy Pose with your elbows bent and your hands facing each other in front of your chest. Your hands will be three to four inches apart.

   A. Twist to the left side and clap your hands. Return to the starting position at the center, but do not clap. Twist to the right side and clap. Return to the center but do not clap. Continue in this manner for 2 1/2 Minutes.

Close your eyes and continue the movement with your eyes closed. 1 1/2 Minutes.

   B. Begin chanting "Har" at each position. Chant "Har" as you clap left and chant "Har" as you come to center and do not clap, Chant "Har" as you clap right, and chant "Har" as you return to center and do not clap. Chant and move at the rate of two "Har's" per second. 6 Minutes.

Inhale, hold your breath for 15 seconds, and then relax.

Mantra to Open up Blockages in Your Life

August 4, 1975

One day Yogi Bhajan told his students, *"Now suppose something happens (in) your life which you want to move and it's not moving. There is a block, which you want to move, and it's not moveable...then chant 'Aad such, jugaad such, hai bhay such, nanak hosee bhay such.' It's a lever. It is the biggest lever available to you among mantras."*[1]

"Baba Siri Chand was the eldest son of Guru Nanak (the first Guru of the Sikhs). He was a very detached yogi and lived for one hundred and fifty years. Did nothing but good. His strength is not only miracles, but spontaneous. We have this mantra of his and if you do that, anything which is stopped in your life, it shall flow. There is no power like it on earth. In some circumstances I have seen it make the impossible to become possible very fast."[2]

"Guru Arjun Dev (the fifth Guru of the Sikhs) went to Baba Siri Chand and said, 'Sahibo, I am writing Sukhmani. I am writing the great situation and combination of words that will give people comfort. I want to produce on this earth, everlasting comfort. I have finished the sixteenth pauri of Sukhmani and now it doesn't proceed further. I am stuck. Seventeenth (pauri) I am to write, please say something.'"

"And then Baba Siri Chand said, 'Well, wait a minute, Guru Nanak gave the Guruship to you folks, and it is your problem to write Gurbani, not mine...I just came to bless you. It doesn't mean I have to say Gurbani for you.'"

"And Guru Arjun Dev replied,' No, sir, this writing isn't working for me.' And there Baba Siri Chand wrote: Aad such, jugaad such, hai bhay such, nanak hosee bhay such."(This mantra became the slok of the seventeenth pauri of Sukhmani Sahib.)[3]

Aad such, jugaad such, haiBHAY such,
Nanak hosee BHAY such.

Sit in a comfortable meditative posture with your spine straight and chant this mantra. If you have a recording such as the one found on the Lord of Miracles CD, you can chant along musically.

All that is stopped shall move

---

[1] Excerpt 8/14/91
[2] Excerpt 7/28/94
[3] Excerpts 1/1/89 and 8/4/74

Mudra to Open up Blockages in Communication

November 17, 1989

When Yogi Bhajan taught this mudra, he said, "There are certain techniques that can help you without money…such as, for example, you do not know how to communicate something that is bothering you and you have to go to a meeting to talk."

Press the pad of the thumb firmly onto the nail of the Mercury (pinky) finger for about one minute. When we press the pad of the thumb onto the nail of the Mercury finger, it is called locking the Mercury finger. "By locking with the pinkie of Mercury finger, you develop the inner strength to communicate anywhere with anyone, under any circumstances. Or read the thoughts thereafter."

Then change the mudra and touch the tip of the thumb to the tip of the Mercury (pinky) finger. "It is a total physiological situation. And when you will touch this (the two tips together) and sit, it means your mercury (communication energy) has to be dominating along with your ego. There is no reason that you should not carry the day."

This technique was taught to help us when we don't know how to communicate something that is bothering us. It works equally well when we are trying to communicate some creative work and we are blocked.

"Your entire sense of communication shall come on your command. For that, you don't have to have initiation, you don't have to belong to anybody, and you will carry the day. It's not religious, and it is not non-religious, either. It is a reality that when your ego (thumb) will press on the Mercury finger, it is just telling the horse, 'Baby, let us gallop.'" YB

Knowing What to Do

August 22, 1986

When you do not know what to do, do this. Sit in Easy Pose, interlace your fingers and put them behind your head with your elbows spread wide apart. Start by listening silently to *Har Har Mukande with Affirmations* by Liv Singh Khalsa. Close your eyes and concentrate at your navel as you listen to the affirmations. When the music begins, pump your navel every time you hear "Har." Start with 11 Minutes and work up to 31 Minutes.

"Now listen by both ears, not by one ear. Whatever you listen by one ear, you are just listening. Whatever you hear, you hear by using both ears."
Yogi Bhajan

Sahaj Yoga

January 12, 1976

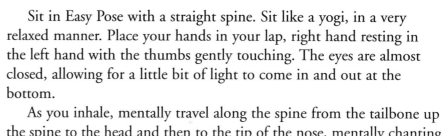

Sit in Easy Pose with a straight spine. Sit like a yogi, in a very relaxed manner. Place your hands in your lap, right hand resting in the left hand with the thumbs gently touching. The eyes are almost closed, allowing for a little bit of light to come in and out at the bottom.

As you inhale, mentally travel along the spine from the tailbone up the spine to the head and then to the tip of the nose, mentally chanting the mantra "Mahan Kal."

As you exhale mentally travel from the tip of the nose back down along the spine to the tailbone, mentally chanting the mantra "Kal Ka." A white radiance may be envisioned along the spine as the breath travels up and down. (Like the mercury rises in a thermometer, the divine power rises in the spine as you inhale. As you exhale the divine power goes back down into the tailbone.)

"Happiness is not in wealth. Happiness is in your values... Be contained, content, and conscious... that's happiness."
YB

Mahan Kal
Kal Ka
Translation:
Great Flow of Being
Flow of Eternal Power (the Kundalini)

Inhale — MAHAN KAL
Exhale — KAL KA

Begin by practicing this meditation for 11 Minutes. At the finish, inhale, raise the arms up over the head and vigorously shake your hands. Relax, stretch the arms up once again, and shake the hands rapidly. Relax.

This meditation was practiced by Guru Gobind Singh (the Tenth Sikh Master) three hundred years ago. Any person, in any non-improved state of mind, body, and soul can rise to any level of consciousness by doing this. Get into it. With a little practice you will always be in a state of bliss. Establish the rhythm.

Mantra to Make the Blind See

55

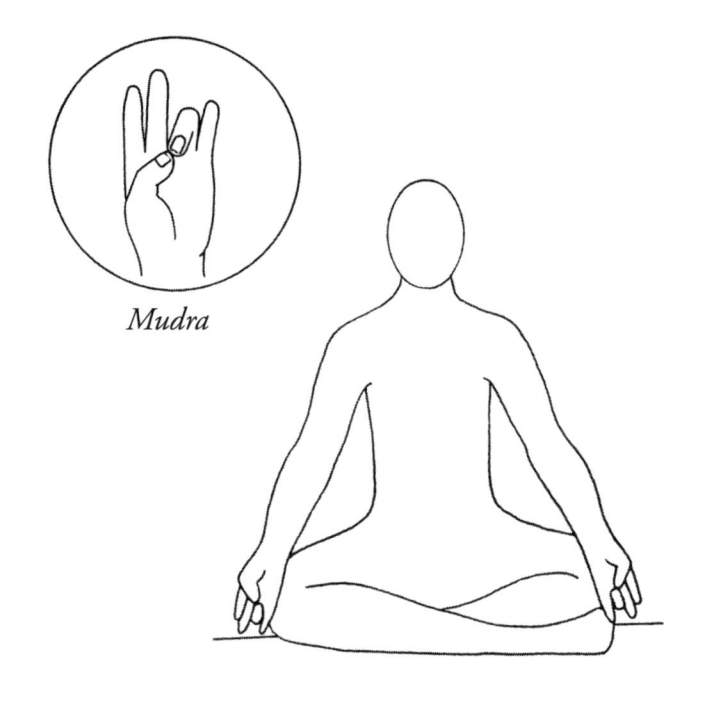

Mudra

Maha Kal Sat
Hari Gobind Nanak

Translation:
Great flow of being, wherein dwells Infinite Truth,
The sustaining power of God's creativity takes us beyond negativity.

Sit in a comfortable meditative posture with your spine straight.
Bring each hand into Surya mudra: the tip of the thumb is touching the tip of the Sun (ring) finger. Focus your eyes at the tip of your nose. The mantra is chanted in the same form and rhythm as the original "Raa Maa Daa Saa, Saa Say So Hung" meditation.
11 Minutes.

"Wisdom, character, and consciousness conquer everything."

YB

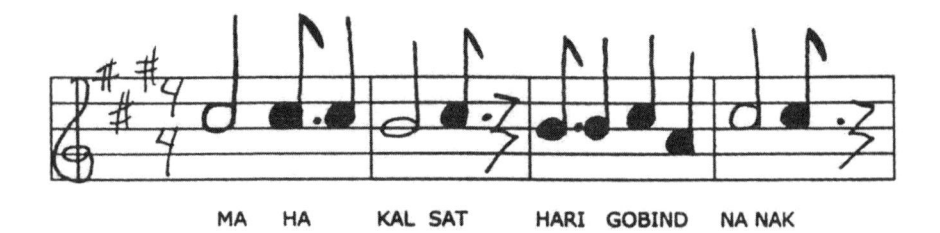

MA HA   KAL SAT   HARI GOBIND   NA NAK

(This meditation was privately taught. It was checked for accuracy with Yogi Bhajan in June, 2003)

Balancing the Projection with the Intention

April 22, 1976

Sit in a comfortable meditative posture with your spine straight and your chin in and chest out. Bend your elbows and bring your hands up to the level of your heart center in a very natural way, with the palms flat and facing upward. Keep your elbows relaxed by your sides. Spread your fingers apart (but do not spread them wide) and spread your thumb back from your hand as well. Keep the fingers spread apart but relaxed,

Keep the palms up and touch the tips of the Sun (ring) fingers together. The Mercury (pinkie) finger of the right hand goes under the Mercury finger of the left hand. They do not touch, but form a ninety-degree angle to each other.

Close your eyes and chant Saa-Taa-Naa-Maa in the traditional manner of Kirtan Kriya. *(Focus at your brow point, using the "L" form of meditation: imagine that there is a constant flow of energy from the Crown Chakra at the top center of your head down into your head and out your Third Eye Point to Infinity. For example, as you chant "Saa," the "S" sound begins at the top of your head and the "aa" ends at the brow point as it is projected to Infinity. The "L" shape follows the energy pathway called the Golden Cord, the connection between the pineal and pituitary glands.)*

Saa   Taa

Naa   Maa

As you chant "Saa," tense the tips of your thumbs and the tips of your two Jupiter (index) fingers. As you chant "Taa," tense the tips of your thumbs and the tips of your two Saturn (middle) fingers. As you chant "Naa," tense the tips of your thumbs and the tips of your two Sun (ring) fingers. As you chant "Maa," tense the tips of your thumbs and the tips of your two Mercury (pinkie) fingers. Keep your hands still, they do not move as the fingertips are tensed. One complete cycle of Saa-Taa-Naa-Maa takes almost five seconds. Let your breath adjust itself.

Begin by practicing this kriya for 11 Minutes and gradually increase the time up to 31 Minutes.

You may find that it is difficult to exactly stimulate the correct fingers. Be patient with yourself, because this is a process of consciously developing control of the neural pathways between the brain and the fingers in coordination with the mantra. The intention is to tense the fingertips and the expression is how precisely and well the fingertips respond. Stay with it and you will find deep peace of mind.

SA   TA   NA   MA

Yogic scriptures tell us of the four stages of the mind: normal awareness, the dream state, total mental rest, and total awareness. Mastery of this meditation enables the practitioner to master these four levels of the mind. It can create a mental equilibrium so that our expression will be consistent with our intention.

"If you cannot find balance in your existence, nothing in your life will ever have any meaning to you."
— YB

Sa-Ta-Na-Ma Meditation, the Second Phase

September 4, 1996

This is the second phase of the Kirtan Kriya, the Saa-Taa-Naa-Maa Meditation. It will invoke in you your third eye, through which you can see all and what there is. You will be able to know right from wrong in a split second. If you can see through your third eye, you can know what another person is actually saying, doing, and projecting toward you. You will be able to totally analyze life and avoid problems.

Sit in Easy Pose with your spine straight, with your chin in and chest out. Your elbows are bent and by your sides. Bring your hands in front of the center of your chest, fingers pointing straight ahead, palms facing each other about four inches apart. The fingers are relaxed and slightly spread apart. Close your eyes.

Tap the thumbs and Jupiter (index) fingers of the two hands together, mentally reciting "Saa" as they touch. And then separate them.
Tap the thumbs and Saturn (middle) fingers of the two hands together, mentally reciting "Taa" as they touch. And then separate them.
Tap the thumbs and Sun (ring) fingers of the two hands together, mentally reciting "Naa" as they touch. And then separate them.
Tap the thumbs and Mercury (pinkie) fingers of the two hands together, mentally reciting "Maa" as they touch. And then separate them.

"It is not these two eyes which matter in life, It is not this head which matters in life. It is not your talk which matters in life. What matters is that your projection carries your personality, character, and spirit with a precision and penetration."

YB

Saa

Taa

Naa

Maa

The movement is done to the rhythm of *Punjabi Drum Music: the Dance Beat* tape. Continue for 16 Minutes. For the last 45 Seconds of practice, open your eyes and watch your fingers. Make sure that your speed, your projection, and your mental recitation are correct.

To finish: inhale deeply, hold the breath for 10 seconds and sit with your touch. Exhale. Inhale again, hold the breath 15-20 seconds, and feel the five energies of your fingers being consolidated into your fiber. Exhale. Inhale, hold the breath 15 seconds while you meditatively concentrate on the energy flow in each pair of fingers individually. Exhale. Relax.

Panj Graani Kriya
Open the Diaphragm to Change Yourself Inside and Out

January 2, 1996

This meditation (from what Yogi Bhajan called the "half angle" system) is a part of an ancient science that is very old, very sacred, and very simple. It was kept for the higher caliber of disciples. When a student became a siddh and was certified and qualified, then his teacher would give him certain exercises of this caliber. These exercises are for those who have qualified themselves as sages with discipline and with spirit.

Sit in Easy Pose with your spine straight and your chin in and your chest out. Bend your right elbow and bring your right hand in front of your face with the palm facing left and the fingers slightly spread. The tips of the fingertips are level with your brow point.

Place your left hand against your right hand so that each finger of the left hand touches the mound at the base of the corresponding finger of the right hand. (The Jupiter (index) finger of the left hand touches the base of the Jupiter (index) finger on the right hand and so on.) Your left thumb locks around the right wrist. This mudra creates an energy bond.

Make an "O" shaped mouth and begin Breath of Fire through your mouth. Create a strong and rhythmic breath. Your eyes will close down automatically. 11 Minutes.

To finish: Inhale, hold the breath for 15 seconds, press your hands together with the maximum power you have. Exhale. Inhale, hold the breath for 15 seconds, press your hands together, pushing both hands with equal pressure. Exhale. Inhale, hold your breath for 15 seconds, keep the hands pressed together as you twist once to the left as far as you can, then twist once to the right as far as you can, then return to the center, and exhale. Relax.

If you practice this kriya for forty days, it can change you inside and out. But there is a note of warning: no matter how good it feels, do not practice it for more than 11 Minutes.

This kriya works on the diaphragm muscle. When the diaphragm muscle is open, flexible, and correctly tuned, it's physical and energetic action can keep the body in a state of health that prevents heart attacks and brain hemorrhages.

(After five minutes of practice, you may find that you have pain in your diaphragm area. This can indicate that your diaphragm muscle is out of shape, because you have not the habit of breathing from your lower abdomen. Because of this, your lower lungs are clogged up and your blood does not have a high oxygen capacity. This kriya will cause the body to regularize itself and the sensation of this may be painful. The last two minutes of the kriya, your nervous system may get itchy, but just go through it.)

" Mind has a power over matter. If the Self is tuned to a high frequency and the respectabilty of Self is within one's own honor, there is nothing in the world one cannot move. One can move mind, material, and time. These three things the human has the power to develop himself to control: mind, matter, and time."

YB

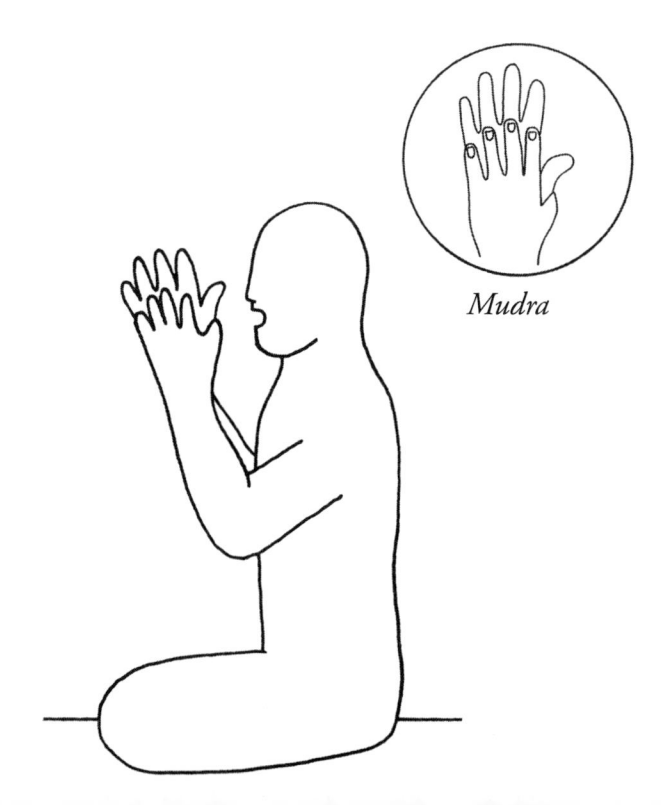

Mudra

Prosperity, Fulfillment, and Success
Circling your Psyche

January 23, 1993

If you do this meditation correctly, you will experience the rising of your own consciousness.

Sit in Easy Pose with your weight balanced equally on both hips. Keep your spine straight. Your elbows are bent with your arms close to your sides and your hands pointing upward. The Jupiter (index) finger is extended straight up and the rest of the fingers are curled into a fist, locked down with the thumb.

Move your hands in small, rapid outward circles while keeping the elbows close to the sides of your body. Close your eyes and chant "Har, Haray, Haree" with the tip of your tongue. Chant at a rate of approximately one repetition of the mantra per second. Move the hands quickly.
11 Minutes.

To finish: continue circling your Jupiter fingers as rapidly as possible but change the chant to "Har, Har, Har, Har." Do this for 15 Seconds and relax.

"You determine your worth. Nobody else can do it. Whatever worth you give yourself, that shall be."

YB

Pranic Meditation for the Heart Center

April 3, 1996

This pranic meditation with the triangle mudra of the Jupiter fingers works very intensely on the heart center. It can keep your brain in good shape, provided that your breath is long and deep and conscious.

1

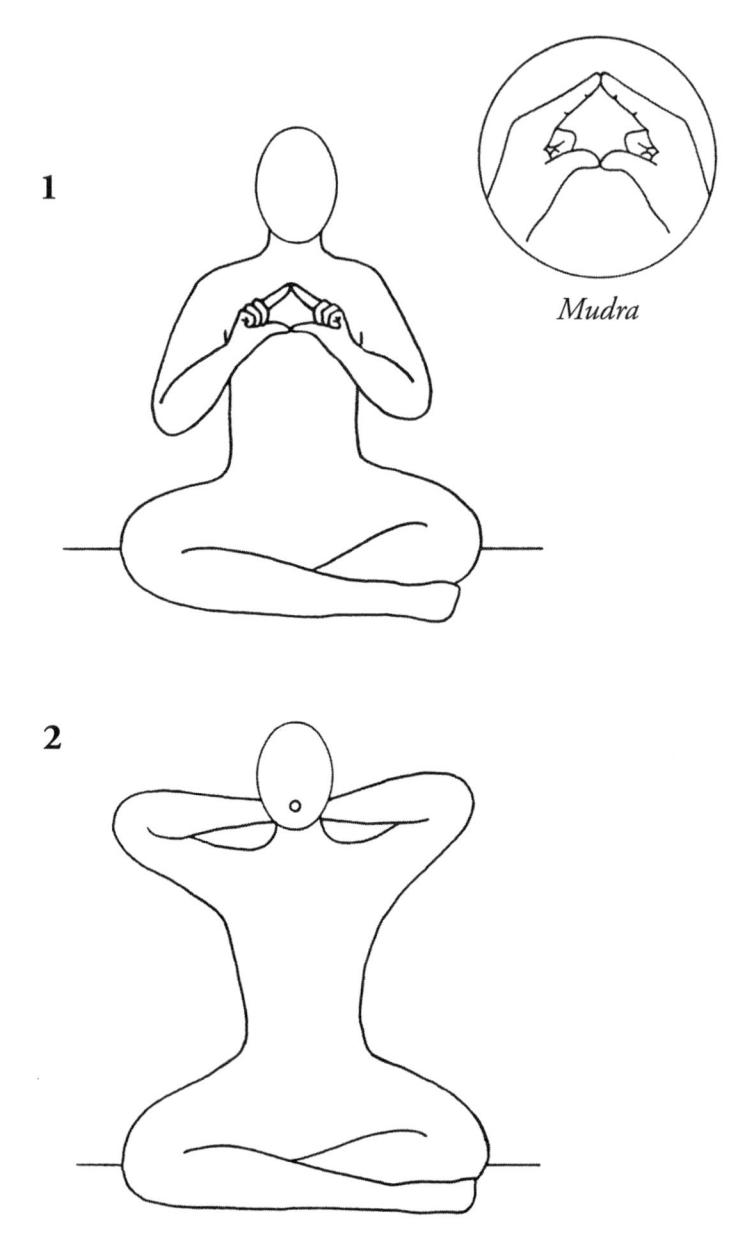

Mudra

2

1. Touch the Jupiter (index) finger and thumb of your right hand to the Jupiter finger and thumb of your left hand, creating a triangle-shaped space between the two Jupiter fingers. *(The better the triangle you can make, the better will be the effect of the meditation.)* Curl the other fingers of each hand into the palm, like you are using just those three fingers to make a fist.

Place this mudra at the center of your chest, in front of your heart center. Close your eyes. Begin consciously breathing long, slow, and deep. Concentrate very deeply on your breathing; do not use automatic breathing.

As you inhale imagine that the breath is enriching you by bringing a lot of energy to you. As you exhale imagine the breath carrying away all of your weaknesses. Breathe with the awareness of the real living prana in each breath. Continue for 14 1/2 Minutes. *(At about 5 1/2 minutes into the meditation, you will enter a twilight zone and you must steady your concentration on the pranic breath. At about 8 1/2 minutes, your body may start to feel itchy and your nervous system may try to interfere with your concentration. Stay steady and go through it.)*

2. Then quickly interlock your hands around the back of your neck, make an "O" shape of your mouth, and begin breathing rapidly and deeply through the "O" mouth for 1 Minute. The faster and deeper you make this breath, the more healing you will create for yourself. Get out whatever dis-ease is within.

Inhale deeply and immediately exhale with a whistle, whistling all your breath out. Once again inhale deeply and immediately exhale with a whistle, whistling all your breath out. Last time: inhale deeply, hold your breath for 20 seconds and squeeze every muscle in your body, spreading energy to every molecule by your own will and power. Exhale.

"Every word spoken must go to the heart, that is the art."

YB

3

3. Relax for about a minute.

4. Then, to return yourself to normal, make claws of your hands, contracting and releasing your hands like a cat scratching. 1 1/2 Minutes. This small action balances the polarities and shows how much we can change ourselves by doing simple little things. Take some time to talk and socialize for another 1-2 Minutes so you can be sure you are ready to resume normal activity. (If you are practicing by yourself, then relax on your back for 1-2 minutes.)

The first morning after you do this meditation, have a glass of fresh lemon juice and water ready by your bedside. When you arise for the day, sip this drink very slowly. This will seal the meditation. (Rinse out your mouth afterward to protect the enamel of your teeth from the acid in the lemon juice.)

The chakras are the transmission gears of the mental body. When they cannot adjust to the pressure of the times, you start slipping gears, and then your caliber starts slipping. Your alertness is not there to serve you.

The third chakra, at the navel point, is a border area where our lower and upper parts meet. It is a twilight zone of the body. There are two such twilight zones: the third chakra and the sixth chakra. This kriya builds the inner strength of the third chakra. Master this meditation and you won't lose your youth and your chakra gears will serve you well.

1

2

3

Working on the Third Chakra

March 27, 1997

1. Sit in Easy Pose with your spine straight. Extend your arms straight out in front of you and roll your arms inward at the shoulders to bring the backs of the hands together. The arms extend straight out from the shoulder, parallel to the floor, with the backs of the hands touching.

Look at the tip of your nose. Hold this position for 1 1/2 Minutes and then begin Breath of Fire, powerfully pumping your navel point. Breathe from the navel not from the nose. Hammer the navel in rhythm to *Tantric Har* by Simran Kaur Khalsa. Continue for 4 1/2 Minutes.

2. Stretch the arms out to the sides. Right palm faces upward to the heavens. Left palm faces downward to the earth. Keep the arms stretched out straight with no bend in the elbows and begin bouncing the arms up and down just a little (approximately a four-inch total range of movement). Chant Har with *Tantric Har,* chanting from the navel and bouncing the arms in rhythm with the chanting. Make sure that you vigorously pump the navel to produce the mantra. The arm movement and the navel pumping must balance. 4 1/2 Minutes. This part of the exercise will uplift you and make you strong.

3. Bring your hands into prayer pose at the center of your chest. Calm yourself and slow down your breathing. Inhale as slowly as you can, hold the breath as long as you can, and exhale as slowly as you can. Let the energy circulate. Meditatively listen to Nirinjan Kaur's recording of *Every Heartbeat.* 7 1/2 Minutes.

To finish: inhale, hold your breath for 25 seconds, and press your palms together with twenty-five pounds of pressure. Tighten the whole body so that the energy can play through every rhythm of the nerves, muscles, and tissues. Exhale like cannon fire. Inhale again, hold the breath 20 seconds, and again press the palms together with the utmost pressure so that you can feel your chest expanding. Cannon fire out your exhale. Last time, inhale, hold your breath for 15 seconds, pressurize your body. Exhale and relax.

"Those who practice discipline have to be very generous to themselves. Discipline should never be rigid. Discipline should be self-acknowledging, so that you can go along with it."

YB

Working on the Fourth, Fifth, and Sixth Chakras

March 25, 1997

Mudra

This kriya will change your chakras and make you better able to move through your chakra system. This will make you a better human being.

1. Sit up straight like a yogi. Keep your eyes open and look straight ahead. Use your thumb to tightly lock down your Mercury (pinkie) and Sun (ring) fingers of each hand. Extend the Jupiter (index) and Saturn (middle) fingers up straight.

Bend your elbows. Press your elbows and upper arms very tightly against your rib cage. This balance of force will consolidate your position so that when the hands revolve, your whole body will move. Revolve your hands rapidly in circles at a rate of three circles per second. Keep moving, don't stop. 5 1/2 Minutes.

Correctly and rapidly doing the movement will cause the spine and neck to loosen up and get adjusted. It will cause the armpits to sweat, which will release toxins from the brain.
Eleven minutes of this exercise done correctly every day is good for your heart.

2. Stretch your arms out straight to the sides. Right palm faces upward to the heavens; left palm faces downward to the earth. Allow no bend in the elbows. Close your eyes and look at the tip of your nose. Let the body balance itself. Become solid like stone. Don't move. 6 Minutes.

This position creates a balanced magnetic field between the earth (left hand facing downward) and the heavens (right hand facing upward). You must stay steady. The temptation to move can become very strong. Go through the discomfort so that you can train your brain to overcome pain by issuing its own natural pain reliever. Open up this channel and you can train yourself to conquer pain.

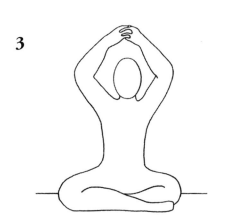

3. Inhale and interlock your fingers. Lift your arms up to form a circle over the top of your head, like an aura. Exhale. Hold this position and whistle along with the instrumental version of *Ardas Bhaee* on the recording called *Healing Sounds of the Ancients #5* for 6 Minutes.
To finish:
   Inhale, hold the breath for 15 Seconds, while you keep your fingers interlaced and stretch your arms up so high that you lift up your entire body. At the same time, expand your rib cage outward. Exhale.
   Inhale, hold the breath for 10 Seconds, repeating the stretch upward, while opening your chest cavity as wide as possible. Exhale.
   Last time: inhale, hold the breath 10 Seconds and slowly and strongly twist to the left and slowly and strongly twist to the right. Return to the center, exhale, and relax.

"Serve people. Don't expect results. Don't put your harpoon into another person. Just serve. People will love you. It will be an everlasting friendship."

YB

The Magic Mantra

April 26, 1976 Excerpts

"Ek Ong Kar, Sat Gur Prasaad is most powerful of all mantras. There is not anything equal to it, nor can anything explain it. Ek Ong Kar, Sat Gur Prasaad is a pritam mantra, the entire Siri Guru Granth Sahib is nothing but an explanation of this mantra. It is so strong that it elevates the self beyond duality and establishes the flow of the spirit. This mantra will make the mind so powerful that it will remove all obstacles.

"We call it the "magic mantra" because its powerful effect happens quickly and lasts a long time. But it has to be chanted with reverence in a place of reverence. When you meditate on this mantra, be sure that your surroundings are marked by serenity and reverence and that you practice it with reverence. You can mock any mantra you like except this one, because this mantra is known to have a backlash. Normally mantras have no backlash. When you chant them well, they give you the benefit, but if you chant them wrong, they don't have any ill effect. If they don't do any good, at least they won't hurt you. But, if you chant Ek Ong Kar, Sat Gur Prasaad wrong, it can finish you. I must give you this basic warning. This mantra is not secret, but it is very sacred. So chant it with reverence, write it with reverence, and use it with reverence.

"Normally we chant to God before practicing this mantra. Either chant the Mul Mantra (Ek Ong Kaar, Sat Naam, Kartaa Purkh, Nirbho, Nirvair, Akaal Moort, Ajoonee, Saibhang, Gur Prasaad, Jap: Aad Such, Jugaad Such, Haibhee Such, Nanak Hosee Bhee Such) or the Mangala Charan Mantra (Aad Gureh Nameh, Jugaad Gureh Nameh, Sat Gureh Nameh, Siree Guroo Deveh Nameh) before meditating to prepare yourself." YB

Meditation With the Magic Mantra

April 26, 1976

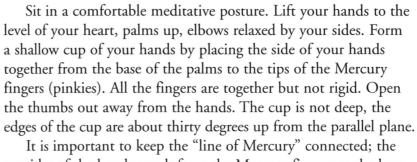
Mudra

Sit in a comfortable meditative posture. Lift your hands to the level of your heart, palms up, elbows relaxed by your sides. Form a shallow cup of your hands by placing the side of your hands together from the base of the palms to the tips of the Mercury fingers (pinkies). All the fingers are together but not rigid. Open the thumbs out away from the hands. The cup is not deep, the edges of the cup are about thirty degrees up from the parallel plane.

It is important to keep the "line of Mercury" connected; the outsides of the hands touch from the Mercury fingers to the base of the palms. Normally there will be no opening whatever, but some people will have a gap between their little fingers. Keep this gap to a minimum.

Close your eyes and look into your hands through your closed eyelids. Chant "Ek Ong Kaar, Sat Gur Prasaad" in a monotone, letting the breath find its own pace. One repetition of the mantra takes between four to five seconds.
31 Minutes.

Begin with three minutes and work slowly up to the full time. Thirty-one minutes of this meditation can keep you in a very elevated state. Practicing this over time can give you a certain stimulation which is beyond explanation. Remember to practice this mantra with reverence in reverent environments at all times.

"Be kind, conscious, and compassionate. The whole world will be your friend."

YB

Using the Magic Mantra as a Gudtkaa to Reverse Negative Energy

July 19, 1982 Excerpts

"In this living nucleus of a psyche, you need inner balance. That is your strength and power. If you don't want to be confused, degraded, upset, or depressed, you need the inner balance. What is that which keeps the inner balance? Shabad. (The sound current.)"

The energy of our lives can be in either a positive balance or a reverse (negative) balance: "For each thought there is an equivalent thought. For each negative thought there is an equivalent positive thought. For each negative scenario there is an equivalent positive one."

"Whether the energy is emotional, commotional, or devotional, it is all praana, right? And it can be reversed."

"When your mind is going berserk, apply a gudtkaa. What is a gudtkaa? It is a stopping lever. (It is found on the water wheel called a Persian Wheel, which is used in the Orient.) It is a lever that can stop you and take the entire weight of the reverse balance. So whenever there is a reverse balance, if you apply the gudtkaa, it will stop it. When the energy is in reverse and it is stopped, it will go to the positive and you'll be good again. Isn't that a simple way to fix yourself?"

And what is the shabad of the gudtkaa? Ek Ong Kaar Sat Gur Prasaad, Sat Gur Prasaad, Ek Ong Kar. It is so written in the book of law, that, if this mantra is chanted five times, it will stop the mind under all conditions and put it in it reverse gear. Five times. Try it any time you want. Your mind may be polluted, dirty, and ugly, but when you chant this mantra, Siri Guru Granth Sahib (the sound current of the Infinite) will sit in your heart. These are not my words, they are the words of Guru Gobind Singh (the Tenth Sikh Master)." YB

(This mantra is generally chanted out loud as a *gudtkaa*, but if circumstances make that impossible, it is also effective when chanted mentally.)

Gudtkaa Kriya

July 19, 1982

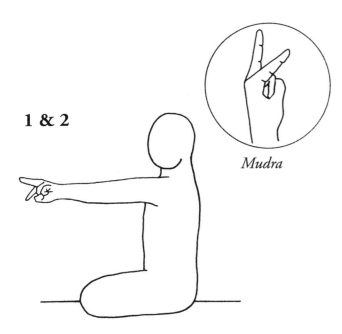

1 & 2

Mudra

3 & 4

1. Sit in Easy Pose with your spine straight. Use the thumb to lock down the Mercury (pinkie) and Sun (ring) fingers. Raise the Saturn (middle) finger up at a diagonal and lower the Jupiter (index) finger down at an angle (like scissors). Stretch your arms straight out in front of you, parallel to the ground, with the palms facing down.

When the Saturn finger is higher and the Jupiter finger is lower and they are on a diagonal to each other, it is called Gudtkaa Kriya.

Close your eyes and concentrate at the Third Eye Point. Begin a brisk continuous chanting of Ek Ong Kaar Sat Gur Prasaad, Sat Gur Prasaad Ek Ong Kaar. One complete recitation of the mantra takes about four seconds. Continue chanting for 11 Minutes.

If you can stretch it tight, put the fingers straight, have the angle right, and concentrate at the Third Eye Point, you will start feeling something. Something will start happening right there. Don't wait for tomorrow, feel it today. Now.

2. Then inhale, hold the position, stretch the arms, stretch the spine, and hold the breath as long as you can. Exhale. (In class the breath was held for over 1 Minute.) Then rapidly and powerfully inhale-and-exhale three times. (Each inhale and exhale takes about three seconds.)

3. Relax and put your hands in your lap. Put your attention at your Third Eye Point and be aware of what is going on there. 1 Minute.

Referring to the Third Eye Point, the yogic scriptures say, " Kamal bigaase, sabh dookh naase. The moment the lotus turns around, all disease and pain go away."

4. Keep your attention at the Third Eye Point and visualize a huge rectangular tank of water surrounded by a marble walkway. Imagine that there is a huge gate on the west side of the walkway. From this gate a bridge goes out to a holy temple in the middle of the tank of water. In the temple music is playing. Hear it and experience it. 2 Minutes.

Inhale deeply, exhale, relax, open your eyes, and bring yourself back to ordinary awareness.

"This is called Pratyahar, the science to control the mind and totally synchronize it. What is the gudtkaa? Pratyahar. What is the mantra of Pratyahar? Ek Ong Kaar, Sat Gur Prasaad, Sat Gur Prasaad, Ek Ong Kaar."

YB

Maha Gyan Agni Kriya

May 20, 1976

Mudra

This is a very powerful kriya. Maha Gyan means "the great knowledge." Agni means the "purity of fire." Practice this kriya unto that infinity of God.

Sit in a comfortable meditative posture, with your spine straight and your chin in and chest out. Cup your hands at heart level with your fingertips touching. Your hands make a "little boat." Make sure that the outsides of the hands from the Mercury (pinkie) fingers all the way to the base of the palms are touching as much as possible. Place your thumbs just inside your hands and bend them down ninety degrees. The thumbs touch each other and your hands. It is a snug position.

Close your eyes. Inhale deeply and chant "Ek Ong Kaar, Sat Gur Prasad, Sat Gur Prasad, Ek Ong Kar" in a monotone eight times in one breath. Begin by practicing this kriya for 11 Minutes and slowly build up to 31 Minutes.

"With your breath, you can touch your soul."

YB

Creating the Mudra

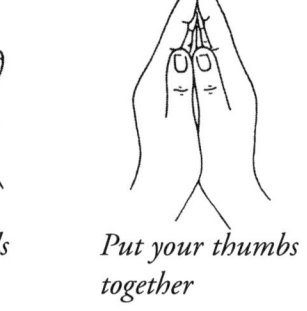

Cup your hands with the sides touching

Put your thumbs together

Bend your thumbs down inside your hands

Mantras

Aad guray nameh, jugaad guray nameh,
Sat guray nameh, siri guroo dayv-ay nameh.

I bow to the primal wisdom. I bow to the wisdom true through the ages.
I bow to the true wisdom. I bow to the great wisdom within.

Aad such, jugaad such, haibhay such, Naanak hosee bhay such.

True in the beginning. True throughout the ages.
True at this moment. Nanak says this shall ever be true.

Ek Ong Kaar, Sat Gur Prasad, Sat Gur Prasad, Ek Ong Kaar.

The Creator and the creation are One. This is experienced by the True Guru's Grace.
This is experienced by the True Guru's Grace that the Creator and the creation are One.

Ek ong kaar, sat naam, kartaa purakh, nirbho, nirvair,
Akaal moort, ajoonee saibhang, gurprasaad. Jap.
Aad such, jugaad such, haibhee such, Nanaak hosee bhee such.

The Creator and all creation are One. This is our True Identity.
God is the doer of all. Beyond fear. Beyond revenge.
Undying form. Unborn. Self-illumined, complete in the Self.
This is realized by Guru's Grace. Repeat the naad.
True in the beginning. True throughout the ages.
True at this moment. Nanak says this shall ever be true.

Gobinday, mukanday, udaaray, apaaray,
Hareeung, kareeung, nirnaamay, akaamay.

Sustainer, liberator, enlightener, Infinite.
Destroyer of evil. Creator, nameless, desireless.

On the pronunciation of the mantra "Har"

The "a" in the mantra "Har" is pronounced like the "u" in "hug."
The "r" is produced in a special way with the tip of the tongue touching the roof of the mouth, just behind the front teeth.
The mantra is chanted by strongly pulling in and up on the navel point, so that, as the air is forced from the lungs, the sound "Har" flows out with the breath, ending as the tip of the tongue touches the roof of the mouth.

Variations on the mantra "Har"

Har

The power of God

Haree

God in creative action

Haray

The manifestation of creation

These three mantras call on various aspects of the Creator and appear in different combinations and with other mantras as well.

Har, Haray, Haree

The Creative Infinity; the Power, the Creative Action, the Completion.

Har Har Mukanday

Powerful creative God, the liberator

Har Har Wha-hay Guroo

Creative God, the ecstasy of Infinite Wisdom.

Haree Raam, Haree Raam, Haree Raam, Haray, Haray

Creative God, more radiant than a million suns
Creative God, more radiant than a million suns
Creative God, more radiant than a million suns
Your brilliant light is manifested in your creation.

Humee humm, toomee toomm, wha-hay guroo.

I am Thine in mine, myself, in the experience of Divine ecstasy.

Jaap Sahib

This is a long prayer in poetic form written by the 10th Sikh Guru, Guru Gobind Singh.
A translation and transliteration can be found in *The Psyche of the Soul* by Siri Singh Sahib Harbhajan Singh Khalsa Yogiji and Bhai Sahiba Bibiji Inderjit Kaur Puri.
It is available through Ancient Healing Ways (see page II).

Mahan kal
Kal ka

Great flow of being,
Flow of Eternal Power (the Kundalini energy)

Maha kal sat
Hari gobind Naanak

Great flow of being, wherein dwells Infinite Truth,
The sustaining power of God's creativity takes us beyond negativity.

Sat naam

Eternal Truth is the essence of all being.

Sat naam, ji.

Eternal Truth is the essence of all being, oh my soul.

Wha-hay Guroo

The experience of Divine Wisdom is ecstasy.

Wha-hay Guroo, wha-hay jio.

The experience of Divine Wisdom is ecstasy. My soul is in ecstasy.